THE ADVENTURES OF HOLLY AMOS

CLINT WESTGARD

ALSO BY CLINT WESTGARD

Published by Lost Quarter Books
www.lostquarterbooks.com

This edition 2017

ISBN: 978-1-928035-34-3

For Mom, who inspired in me a love for both history and the prairies.

CONTENTS

PART ONE

1—MORRIS AND HOLLY

They hit the payroll, catching them in a crossfire as they came into Horseshoe Canyon on their way to pay the miners at the Atlas Coal Mine in Wayne. There were only two guns protecting it, and Morris Danforth and Holly Amos picked one off each from their perches high across the canyon. Clean shots both, right through the chest. The gunfire reverberated around the canyon, sounding almost as though it were coming up behind them.

The two men leading the packhorses tried to flee, but they shot the horses out from under them. If the Atlas Coal men survived their falls, Holly and Morris did not see. They were too busy scrambling to their own mounts to catch up with the fleeing payroll. That they did, intercepting the stampeding horses before they could scamper up the narrow and winding trail that led from the canyon to the plains above.

When they had calmed the panicked animals, they left the canyon behind, heading up into the hills to the north, where they had a camp set up. There were no trees there, just wild prairie, but the hills hid them well enough from anyone passing through on the way to Wayne. The road was little traveled, except by the Atlas Coal Company men, and it would be a day or two—if they were lucky—before anyone chanced upon the ambushed payroll. Time enough for them to rest and be gone from here.

Holly saw to the animals, taking them to a nearby slough for water and putting them in hobbles so they could rest and eat. Morris paid no mind to the animals or to her. He was in a frenzy of delight as he counted out the well-creased bills and coins—over two hundred fifty dollars' worth.

"If we get a good price on the packhorses, we should have nearly three hundred when it's all said and done. No more worries for a while, Holly dear."

He let out a whoop and pulled her in for a kiss. "No more worries, Morris honey," Holly said, as she slipped away from his grasp.

Holly set about to making some dinner for them both, opening tins of beans and divvying up the pemmican they had. They had the beans cold, not wanting to risk a fire, and washed them down with what remained of the rotgut they had exchanged with the Indians by Fort Macleod for the pemmican and some rancid buffalo meat. Morris had spent the following week muttering about that, promising to return south and find those bastards and see that they got theirs.

Holly had learned long ago not to say anything when Morris got some damned foolish idea in his head, for it would turn his ire toward her. Just as when he drained the bottle of whiskey and found himself in an amorous mood, she knew enough not to point out that they needed to be going and putting some distance between them and the dead Atlas Coal men.

Morris was trouble when he drank. He was trouble all around. She had known that from the first. It was why she had left home to go with him.

2—CONSTABLE HESTIN

Constable Clive Hestin of the Northwest Mounted Police had just started down the trail into Horseshoe Canyon when he heard the shots in the distance. Two rifles, he thought. Five shots in all.

He paused a good long while to consider his options before starting his horse forward again. Two against one, with him at the bottom of a canyon, seemed a situation that was likely to end poorly for him. Best to proceed with caution and hope that whoever was shooting was out of the canyon and up onto the prairie by the time he arrived.

One of Gordon Eaton's sons had been the one to bring word of a stranger lurking in the hills north and west of the Horseshoe. That had been the day before yesterday, but Hestin had only now managed to head out to investigate. A cardsharp had been killed in a brawl at the Last Chance Saloon in Wayne the night before, and he had spent the last two days interviewing those present to determine which coal miner had killed him. It was tedious, aggravating work, everyone's memories rendered opaque by alcohol, and he was glad for the opportunity to see who the lurking stranger was.

Now that shots had been fired, new questions came with them. Was the stranger involved in some way? As one of the shooters or one of the shot? Or was he a witness?

No matter the answers, Hestin felt in his bones that it would be a long bloody day.

His intuition was proven correct when, an hour later, he came upon the bodies of the two guns hired to guard the Atlas Coal Mine payroll. Flies had already begun to gather on the corpses as the heat of this summer day reached its full bloom. There were four sets of tracks heading east, and when he followed the two that had turned course back west out of the canyon, he came across the two Atlas Coal Mine employees and their horses. He recognized them both, for they came every month from Calgary with pay for the miners. One man was dead, his neck snapped in his tumble from his horse, while the other breathed shallowly beside his fallen horse.

Hestin looked him over carefully and saw that an arm and leg were both broken, and got to work at setting them both. There were no trees in the canyon, it being in the badlands that stretched along this part of the Red Deer River, so he used bits and pieces from the men's possessions and from the saddles of their horses to fashion splints. The man stirred to consciousness as Hestin moved his broken limbs and gave him some water. With that done, he lifted the man up onto his horse and lashed him to the saddle as best he could.

He started walking west, leading the horse out of the canyon, hoping that he came across one of the dead guns' horses. If not, he would be hard-pressed to make it to Gordon Eaton's ranch before nightfall. He kept his free hand ready near his gun, scanning the bare hillsides of the badlands that surrounded him in the canyon, though he knew it was unlikely the two shooters remained anywhere near. They had come for the payroll, it seemed clear, and had set an ambush. Given he hadn't met them on the way here, they had obviously left the canyon and would be on their way to parts unknown.

Hestin thought it likely that one of the shooters was the stranger Gordon Eaton's son had seen two days before.

The question now was, where would the shooters flee? The answer to that would have to wait until Hestin saw to the Atlas Coal man.

3—PLANS AND DECISIONS

The plan had been to go south, skirting between the western edge of the badlands and Calgary, before heading into the foothills of the Rocky Mountains to make their way to Lethbridge. There they would sell the two packhorses and continue further south, across that amorphous 49th Parallel, and into the United States of America. What happened once they reached Montana was not discussed, but Holly knew exactly what would take place. Morris would gamble and drink and their newfound fortune would not last out the year. The next summer, they would return north again to deal in whiskey and petty thievery.

For a time, Holly had been satisfied with following these, the unchanging seasons of her life, once she had cast her lot with Morris Danforth. But lately her thinking on the matter had changed. The same restlessness that had led her from her family's homestead and into Morris Danforth's arms had returned. She tried to ignore it as best she could, telling herself that Morris treated her decently enough and the adventuring he had promised had materialized, more or less. Her life did not lack for excitement, even if she had not imagined it would be quite so filled with dreary nights spent out on the prairie, trying to keep warm without a fire amid swarms of insects as the coyotes and foxes provided their mournful chorus.

It did not help that Morris was something of a fool, as she had slowly come to realize. At first she had believed he was clever, but that, she now understood, was simply because he had known more of the ways of this world than she. Now she saw him for what he truly was. Never more so than today, when his drinking and amorous advances had led them to leave the hills far later than they should have. They descended to the plains below at the same time the mounted policeman emerged from the canyon with the surviving Atlas Coal man.

At the first sight of the constable, Morris turned and fled back up into the hills. Holly waited a moment, eyeing the man from across the prairie, debating whether she was close enough for a shot with the rifle, before deciding that was foolish in the extreme. Best not to bring the whole mounted police down upon them in a search. She turned her horse about and followed Morris back into the hills, the two packhorses trailing behind her.

She found Morris back by their camp, looking around as though he was lost. "How good a look do you think he got of us?"

"How good a look did you get at him?" Holly said, with an impatient shake of her head.

"He's a mounted policeman," Morris said, his eyes flashing with anger.

"I couldn't pick him out of a firing squad," Holly said, clicking her tongue to start her horse forward. There was no sense lingering any longer. The mounted policeman would, in all likelihood, continue on to whatever ranch or homestead was nearest to see to the injured man lashed to his saddle. But, in the event that he didn't, it seemed prudent to make themselves scarce.

Morris rode up beside her. "Where the hell you going, girl?"

"You want to stick around and wait for the law, you be my guest. I'm leaving."

"Don't you forget who's got the payroll, Holly dear. I'm the one who makes the decisions here."

"Surely you are, Morris," Holly said sweetly, neither stopping, nor glancing in his direction. "Where do you reckon we should head now? Can't go south. Not with the law waiting for us."

Morris was silent for a time, chewing his cud as he mulled the possibilities.

"I've an idea," Holly said. "We could head east a spell. Avoid the badlands, mind. And then head south around Finnegan country. Sell the horses at the first town we come to. Stay to the wild country all the way to Montana."

Morris did not reply, still working over his lip, and Holly knew that he had agreed to her plan. It was the best available, given their circumstances. And once they reached the safety of Montana, she resolved, it would be time to bring their partnership to an end. The next time she and Morris encountered the law, she knew, it would not end so peacefully, and she had every intention of seeing that did not come to pass.

4—CRIMES AND PUNISHMENT

Constable Hestin did not linger at the Eaton Ranch, though it was well into the evening by the time he arrived. He left the Atlas Coal man in Emma's capable hands and took advantage of the long summer day, where the light lasted until nearly eleven in the evening, to head north to where he had encountered the two men responsible for the payroll raid. Before he left, he extracted promises from two of the Eaton boys to leave at dawn the next day. One to go to Wayne to inform the company of their lost payroll and men, and to let them know they would have to see to the bodies. The other to go south and west to Calgary, to notify the NWMP post there of what had taken place and inform them of his next steps.

Those were to head out in pursuit of the two bandits who had attacked the payroll. He provided the Eaton boy with the best descriptions he could to pass on to the Calgary detachment. Two men, both with long hair, neither dark nor blond. Neither wearing anything distinctive that might identify them. One rode a buckskin pony, the other a chestnut. They had been trailing what Hestin supposed were the two payroll packhorses, both paints. They had been too far away for him to gather any other identifying information. The detachment, he knew, would send word by telegraph to the other detachments and towns along the railroad in the territories, so that everyone would be on the lookout for two individuals approximating that description. They would head to a town at some point to sell those two horses. It was just a question of when.

In the meantime, Hestin intended to follow the two bandits. He made his way north up into the hills, where the two had fled when they caught sight of him. There he found the remnants of their camp. It appeared they had been staying there for several days, at least. He took the time to comb the area, for anything they might have left behind that would help to identify them or guide his search, but turned up nothing.

He tried to recall if there had been any strangers visiting Wayne in the last weeks or months. Someone who might have been taking an interest in the way the Atlas Coal Mine handled its payroll. No one came to mind, but that was hardly surprising. There were far too many miscreants and vagrants who made their way to Wayne and took up in one of its saloons or brothels. Some found work in the mine, while others found it in taking the miners' pay from them.

It was one of the drearier postings in the territory. Wayne was a frontier town, with all that implied. The spur-line to the railway had yet to be connected to the new mine, or the growing town, much to the frustration of the Atlas Coal owners. The mine and its coal kept the men— more and more every week it seemed—flush with cash to spend, leading to even more problems. It was a job for a full detachment, not the two men who were left there. One man, really, given that Hestin's superior was a drunken fool who spent most of his days in the detachment house in a blind stupor.

Hestin was left alone to keep the peace, always precarious in such places, which he managed, barely. Any failure to do so would be blamed on him, he knew. As would the ambush, and these murders. The posting had been punishment, a way of ensuring his failure, and a result of the fact that none of his superiors trusted him. Not after he had reported the captain of the Fort Macleod detachment for working with the American whiskey traders to swindle the Blackfoot Indians of the area.

Hestin had no regrets about reporting the man. The Americans were always looking for reasons to sew strife among the Indian tribes of the territory as an excuse for their expansion north. The last thing the NWMP needed was to aid them in the task. He had ignored it for as long as he could, seeing to his duty and keeping the order, until he could do so no longer. The subjection of a dozen Indian squaws to harlotry in service to the captain, spreading syphilis and disease among the traders, had been the final straw.

Hestin pushed these thoughts aside and returned his focus to the two bandits. He needed to find them and bring them to justice, if he was to keep what remained of his career with the mounted police alive. There would be no help from Wayne. Lieutenant Cavanaugh would not raise a flask to aid him. The detachments in Calgary and elsewhere would do little more. He would have to see to the matter himself.

After a few minutes of studying the ground around their campsite, he thought he found their trail. They were heading east. Though the sun was low on the horizon, casting the sky in red, yellow, and violet streaks, he started that way as well, intending to stay on horseback until the light left the day.

5—DOROTHY

The morning following their ambush, Holly started a fire and made coffee at Morris's insistence.

"No way that lawman is following us yet," he said. "He's probably still looking to that coal man."

Holly did not feel quite so certain, but she didn't argue with Morris. He had been angry with her, and no doubt with himself, following their encounter with the law. Any thought of making an easy escape was gone now. They would be on the run until they made it across the border.

They were on horseback before dawn broke, setting a hard pace. They stayed north of the river valley and the badlands, keeping them in sight just on the horizon. The river angled south and they did as well, wandering into the Handhills, until they were north of a village called Dorothy that lay at the edge of the badlands. There, over Holly's objections, Morris rode into town to sell the two packhorses.

"We got to get rid of them Holly, dear," he said, in the exasperated tone of a man who has had to explain things one too many times to a child. "That mounted police saw them for sure. They'll mark us like his uniform, no doubt."

Holly did not disagree with Morris there. But things

had changed now that the law had spotted them. They needed to put as much distance between themselves and him as possible, she felt certain, and to leave as little of a trail behind them as they could. More than that, he had not seen them clearly and could not positively identify them now. But a couple of strangers selling paint packhorses would be remembered. Not many folks came to Dorothy. Not many had reason to.

Better to stay to the wild prairie, away from villages and homesteads, and make their way south. They could sell the ponies closer to Montana, or in the state itself. Make the lawman follow their trail. Holly knew enough of the mounted police to realize they were no Indian scouts. Half of them were drunks and reprobates, little better than the criminals they pursued.

Morris won out, arguing vehemently that this needed to be done. He insisted, as well, that Holly remain outside of town while he negotiated the deal, though he would not say why. Holly knew it was because he didn't want her to know how much money he got for the two ponies. And because he was still angry with her.

When he was upset with her, he became as resentful as a child. Holly knew well enough by now to just let him be. If he wanted the money from the ponies, let him have it. It would all be squandered by him in the end anyway. Even her share. It always was.

She waited for him in the hills above the river valley, where she had a view of whole magnificent prairie. It stretched on to the east, seemingly forever, the horizon never quite ending. Her home lay that direction and she found herself thinking on it, which she rarely did.

Were her parents still well? Had her sister Hettie married? And what of young Harold?

Holly could not count the number of times she had thought to put pen to paper and write them a letter. At least to let them know she was fine and well, as well as could be. But she and Morris never seemed to settle in one place for long enough, so it wasn't as though she could wait for a reply. That was not it, though, she knew. It was more that it would be too difficult to explain why she had left and why she had failed to write until now. And as the years went on, it became harder and harder.

Not that she regretted leaving, not even in the slightest. Tying her fortune to Morris, on the other hand, was something she was thinking on more every day.

He returned by midafternoon, swaying in the saddle, his breath heavy with whiskey. Holly said nothing and they set on their way, heading southeast and following the river.

"We did well, Holly dear," Morris said, after they had ridden some miles in silence.

"I'm sure we did, Morris honey," she said, and smiled.

He nodded, wetting his mustache with his bottom lip. "Yes, we did well, indeed. Got rid of the horses at a fine price and now we can proceed at ease. That lawman won't be able to track us. They just stay up in their forts anyway, dealing with their whores."

Holly nodded, but did not say anything. She knew by his bluster that Morris had unloaded the horses for a song. Yet another thing that would be remembered in a place like Dorothy.

It would do no good to challenge him on the matter, and she did not. He prattled on for the remainder of the afternoon, telling her stories of his time with Buffalo Bill's Wild West show she had heard dozens of times before. When he thought she wasn't looking, Morris stole drinks from a bottle he had acquired in Dorothy. He fell asleep by the fire almost as soon as they were done eating supper, and Holly was left alone to watch the encroaching darkness and the numberless stars above.

It was the next day that they caught sight of the mounted policeman on their trail.

6—FINNEGAN FERRY

Clive Hestin first caught sight of the bandits two days after his initial encounter, cresting a rise on the horizon's edge. After that, they appeared and disappeared ahead of him, depending on the nature of the ground they were riding on. They had to have seen him too, but they had yet to change course in any way—still riding at the same pace and following the river southeast, while skirting the northern edge of its valley. He had not changed his pace either, knowing he could follow their trail wherever they went and preferring to force them into the first move.

He was unsure why they hadn't to this point. They outnumbered him, and all it would take was for them to split up to force him into a difficult choice. There was also the ever-present danger of an ambush. These men were killers, he could not forget. Fortunately, the land here, east of the Handhills, was flat and rolling, a hard place for anyone to hide. Which led him to wonder why they had not descended into the river valley, where the trees and the hillside would provide cover for an attack, while the river could be used to obscure their trail and slow down his pursuit.

It was only as they neared Finnegan and the ferry

crossing there that they turned into the river valley. Hestin followed them with caution, suspecting a trap. Surely they had noticed him following in the distance. The scarlet red of his uniform was unmistakable.

There was a trail leading down to the ferry crossing, well marked and well traveled by traders on their way to Gem, Rosemary, or Duchess in the south, Dowling Lake, Comet, or Rumsey in the north. Few passed by on any given day, though, Hestin knew, so the trail was likely to be empty. The two bandits might very well still be waiting for the ferry to cross over to them by the time he arrived. More likely, they were lying in wait somewhere along the trail to attack him.

After pondering his options, Hestin proceeded down the trail, his eyes alert to the surrounding hills, where someone might position themselves to get a shot at him. The trail ahead was open and empty, and soon he could see the entire sweep of the valley. There were trees lining the banks in places, but where the ferry was pulled across it had been cleared. Hestin could see the flat-topped barge was on his side of the river and could make out several figures milling about on the deck.

His eyes were drawn to one standing in the middle of the boat holding the reins of two horses. One buckskin. One chestnut.

Hestin pulled his horse to a halt on the trail and studied the other two men on the boat. They appeared to be ferrymen, readying to pull at the rope strung across the river. Which meant there was another man somewhere who had Hestin in his sights. He scanned the trail ahead and could see no obvious hiding places. The hills on this side of the river would provide cover, but he thought they were too far for anyone but the finest shot to make an attempt. And there had been better opportunities to shoot him on his descent. Now, if the man shot and missed, Hestin would stand between him and ferry.

That left the trees on the bank, and that was where he

turned his attention, pulling out his eyeglass to better peer within those shadows. As he did, a shot sang across the valley, followed by another. The air stung his cheek as the second bullet hissed by. His horse, doing its training proud, stood its ground, not reacting to the blasts.

Hestin leapt off the back of the horse and dove to the ground, keeping it between him and the river. He swore under his breath that he had not had the foresight to have his rifle free so that he could reply to this assault in kind. Instead, all he had was the revolver at his hip, which was useless at this distance.

Another shot hit the earth in front of the horse, sending a cloud of dust in the air. Hestin had the location of the shooter by then, and he pulled the eyeglass back up to peer into the trees where he was sure the shots had come from. He was in time to see the back of a retreating form, heading through the brush to the ferry. Seeing his chance, Hestin stood up behind his horse and pulled his own rifle from the saddle, moving to lie in front of his still-placid mount.

There were shouts from the ferry from the bandit who remained there. Whether they were directed at Hestin, his counterpart, or the ferrymen, he could not tell. He peered through the eyeglass again and saw the bandit gesturing at the ferrymen to begin pulling the rope, a revolver in his hand. He had a full beard and head of hair, neither of which had been trimmed, combed, or washed in some time, by the look of him. His clothes were grubby and worn.

The ferry began to pull away before the other bandit had arrived, and he had to leap across to reach it, nearly falling into the river as he did. He stayed sprawled on the ferry deck, not even lifting his head as his partner berated him and the ferrymen pulled the boat across the river. Eventually he rose and went to stand at the far end of the deck, his back to Hestin and the horse between them.

Hestin contemplated taking a shot at one of the

bandits' horses or the men themselves, but decided he couldn't risk it with the ferrymen on board. Instead he remained where he was with his eyeglass trained on the deck, hoping to catch a glimpse of the other bandit's face. The man was careful, though, to keep his horse positioned where it blocked Hestin's view, and, as the ferry docked on the other side, he made certain to mount the animal in such a way that Hestin caught only a glimpse of what appeared a young, clean-shaven face.

The other man ordered the two ferrymen off the boat, binding their wrists with a bit of twine. He looked up at where Hestin lay on the ground, pulled out his rifle, and let off two shots, both of them landing harmlessly below. The other bandit shouted something at him, and the bearded man turned to the ferry ropes, drew out a knife, and started to saw through them.

Seeing that, Hestin decided he had to act. He stood and raised his rifle and took careful aim at the bandit, trying to make sure he missed to his far side, away from where the two ferrymen were bound. His first shot missed, but the second one caught the man in one of his arms, sending him spinning to the ground. The other bandit gave a shout, and the bearded man scrambled to his horse and they fled up the trail. Hestin watched them go before he too climbed on his horse, rode down to the river, and began the hard work of pulling the ferry across.

7—CYPRESS HILLS

Morris had been a damned fool to think the mounted policeman would be stupid enough to fall into their ambush at the ferry. He would have been expecting something of the kind the moment he first laid eyes on them ahead on the trail. And yet, Holly was forced to admit, he nearly had fallen into the trap. He very nearly had.

Morris had been furious with her for the shots, accusing her of deliberately missing. Holly had responded with spittle-flecked rage. Never mind that it was true. Morris didn't need to know that. He shouldn't even suspect it, though he would. There had been little to no wind and the sun had been behind her. That was a shot she made if she wanted to.

She had not because she did not want the entire mounted police on their tails as they made their way south. So far there was only this one gallant, and so long as they kept away from any settlements, it would hopefully remain that way. There was also the certainty that Morris would sell her out in a second if he thought he could pin the murder of a constable on her and escape the noose. Not that she could blame him; she would do exactly the same.

The ball lodged in his shoulder had done little to improve Morris's humor. He had been irritable and feverish for the last day, accusing her of being contrary, even as he argued with her every suggestion and refused to let her tend to his wound.

"Maybe you'll miss the ball and take out my heart instead," he remarked on more than one occasion, until Holly simply let the matter drop. It was his life, after all.

Only when the first chills of a fever began to set in did he at last relent and agree with Holly that they needed to find somewhere to hole up while the wound was dealt with. They were near the Cypress Hills by then, an oasis of towering, forest-covered ridges, a world apart from the plains they had just ridden across. The land would provide more than enough cover for them, and with Fort Walsh abandoned, there was little chance of their encountering any mounted police. If they were lucky, they might even take refuge in a trapper's cabin.

They rode up into the hills on the afternoon of their second day from the ferry and their failed ambush. There had been no sign of their pursuer since Finnegan, but Holly did not doubt he was somewhere behind them, following their trail. Unlike so many of the mounted police they had encountered, he knew a thing or two about tracking, and he would be able to follow them up into the hills wherever they went. She could only hope they were not waylaid here so long that he had time to catch up.

By nightfall, they had climbed deep into the hills, and they came across a trapper's cabin near Elkwater Lake, which gave them a clear view of the surrounding territory. Holly was reassured. The constable would not be able to surprise them now. She tied the horses up behind the cabin, where they would be out of sight of anyone approaching from the west, and went to tend to Morris's injury.

"Oh, Holly dear, don't be so cruel," he complained, as she set about removing the ball from his arm. "What I wouldn't give for a sup of whiskey."

"You might have had some, if you hadn't supped it all before we got to Finnegan," Holly said.

"Don't take that tone with me, girl. If you had made those shots, like we both know you can, I wouldn't be in this state."

"What's with this shouting? Are you trying to raise every mounted policeman between here and Enchant?" Holly said.

"Don't you be telling me what to do, girl. If it weren't for me, you'd still be a poor nothing in some pissant town in the far territories. If I want to yell, I'll damn well do it."

Holly did not respond, pursing her lips in concentration. The ball had settled deep into the flesh in Morris's shoulder, but otherwise had done little damage. Digging it out was likely to cause a great deal more, but she had little choice. She couldn't leave it in there, not when it was becoming infected. And because Morris had drunk all the whiskey, she had nothing to clean the wound or the knife she was using to cut him open with. All she could do was risk a fire, boil a little water, set the blade in it, and hope it would be enough.

As she began to dig away, working the blade in deeper and deeper, Morris began to curse her, sweat streaming down his brow. "Goddamn you, Holly girl. Goddamn you. I know you missed that shot on purpose. I know it."

"Don't be a fool, Morris," Holly said, her concentration on working the ball loose.

"Goddamn you. Goddamn you," Morris said, jerking his arm free. "You're fixing to kill me."

"Don't be a fool. And sit still. We have to get the ball out of there, or you will be dead."

"I've known it. Oh, I've known it, Holly dear," Morris said, oblivious of Holly. "You think you're so damned clever. Well, I know what you're up to. You've been fixing to leave me, one way or another, for a while now. Don't think I don't know. And don't think I'm going to let you, either. You're mine, girl. I plucked you off that homestead, and I'll be damned if you go anywhere without my say-so."

Without even glancing up at him, Holly reversed the knife she held, bringing the shaft down upon Morris's nose. He let out a yelp of surprise.

"If you don't stop your moaning, I'll leave you here now for the mounted police to find you. Now quit your crying and let me get this done."

Morris glared at her, his lips quivering in anger, but he held his tongue and let her return to working on his shoulder. She would pay for that blow later, Holly knew. Pay in blood, most likely. It was also disconcerting that Morris suspected she was intending to leave. Perhaps he was not so much the fool she had believed.

Those were concerns for another day. For now, she turned her mind to the ball in his shoulder. On her third attempt, she managed to work it free. She pressed some cloth she had torn from one of her shirts to stanch the wound and bandaged it with one of Morris's, both of which she had cleaned a little with the water she had boiled. They would need to find some whiskey soon to set her mind at ease about the wound. It was still likely to fester.

When she was done stitching up his wound with a little thread, Morris fell into an anguished sleep, his face contorted into a grimace and his brow glistening with a sheen of sweat. She studied him, thinking about their times together and the days that lay ahead. If he suspected her plans to leave him, she would need to plan more carefully for when the moment came. It felt as though it would be coming soon, sooner by the day.

While Morris slept, Holly dug through his satchel and his clothes and removed some of their payroll score. Enough to keep her going for a time, but not so much that he would notice unless he thought to check. Which he might, given his doubts about her. It was a chance she had to take.

As he slept on, she worked feverishly, loosening some patches on her jacket and in her pants. When the patches were loose, she folded the bills and sealed them into her clothes, taking care to make sure there were no telltale bulges or creases. With that done, she went through the cabin to see if the trapper had left them any food—a pressing need, given they had exhausted their meager supplies the day before. There was none, and she was forced to go to bed hungry, curling up alongside Morris, who had begun to snore loudly.

She spent a restless night beside him, troubled by doubt and visions of firefights with the mounted police. The next morning, they awoke to discover the trapper's cabin was surrounded.

8—SERGEANT WEATHERS

"Now you'll see some real police work, constable," Sergeant Weathers said, his breath heavy with liquor.

They were sitting below the trapper's cabin, nearly a dozen men on horseback, including Clive Hestin, all of them drawn by the smoke from the cabin that had signaled the presence of the two bandits the day before. Hestin had followed them into the Cypress Hills, only to come across Weathers and his posse, coming down from Fort Empress, near the confluence of the South Saskatchewan and Red Deer rivers.

"I'm sure, sir," Hestin said, with a nod.

Weathers gave him a mocking smile in return. The mounted police at Fort Empress had been notified of the bandits by the telegraph the Eaton boys had arranged. A further telegraph, notifying them of one of the bandits, matching the description provided by Hestin, selling the two payroll horses in Dorothy, had come a day later. Weathers had surmised the bandits must be heading southeasterly, and had moved to intercept them.

As soon as he came across Hestin, he made clear he was in charge of the operation, going out of his way to make certain that the constable understood his continued presence in the Cypress Hills was conditional upon the sergeant's approval. And he set about ensuring that Hestin found the situation utterly intolerable. Weather's men were slovenly and half-drunk, as was the sergeant, with some of them not even in proper uniform. The sergeant seemed to be daring Hestin to report this to one of the inspectors, knowing that it would get him nowhere. He was one of the superintendent's pets, after all.

It was utterly infuriating, or would have been, if it hadn't been all too familiar. Men like Weathers and situations like this had already resulted in Hestin being dispatched to the most godforsaken posting in the territory. They could do no worse to him, though he knew they would try if he did, as Weathers clearly wanted him to, and reported his actions to his superiors. Who would ignore such reports, as Hestin knew only too well.

Especially if, as seemed likely, they captured the bandits. There had been no sign of anyone in the cabin, the fire having gone out sometime in the evening. One of the scouts Weathers had sent up the hill, under the cover of the brush and trees that blanketed most of it, had said their horses were tied up behind the cabin, which Weathers took as a signal that all was well in hand.

"Put men on the two trails going up the hill," he said. "The rest of us are going up to scare out the grouse. We'll see if they run."

He smirked at Hestin, as though daring him to question his tactics. Hestin did not take the bait, following behind Weathers, along with half of the remaining force, as they started up the hill to the cabin. The rest of the men were left on either side, near the trail that snaked over the hill, in the event that the two bandits somehow slipped through the grasp of those moving up to surround the cabin.

Hestin wondered how badly injured the man he had shot was. It had looked to him as though the bullet had only clipped him, but perhaps it was worse than that. Bad enough to force the two to stop here for a night—

knowing that he was still in pursuit—and tend to it before heading on. It had likely seemed a reasonable risk, given there was only one man in pursuit. They could not have anticipated a dozen more joining the chase, and it was those numbers that seemed likely to seal their fate.

As they crested the hill and approached the cabin, the men fanned out to surround the building. Hestin moved to the rear and saw the two horses, still tied to a lone tree the trapper had left standing when he cleared out the rest of the hilltop. Something about them caught his eye, giving him pause.

On the other side of the cabin, Weathers shouted, "You are surrounded, gentlemen. This is the Northwest Mounted Police. You're wanted for murder and robbery. Surrender yourselves immediately."

The only response to his command was the chirping of the birds in the surrounding trees. Hestin turned away from the cabin to look behind him, scanning the hillside below. It too was covered in brush and trees, except for the trail the trapper had carved, making it difficult to see the three men stationed below, and almost impossible to see if anyone was hidden somewhere in the depths of the foliage. Which, he was almost certain, was the case.

"This is your last chance, gentlemen. We are coming in to arrest you. Surrender yourselves peaceably and I can promise you a fair and honest trial."

Hestin could almost see Weathers' mirthless grin, and had to resist a shudder. The two constables beside him were drawing their pistols and readying to fire. He continued to scan the hill for any sign of the two bandits. They were there somewhere, he knew, hidden within the brush.

"Get ready, damn you," one of the men beside him muttered. "They're about to go in."

Hestin did not turn around. "There's no one in there."

"How the hell do you know?"

"There's no blankets under those saddles," Hestin said,

gesturing toward the bandits' two horses. "They're making a run for it on foot."

"Damn you, I don't care. Our boys are about to go into that building, and we need to be ready to back them up if need be."

Reluctantly, Hestin turned around to face the cabin and drew his revolver. As he turned, he thought he saw a flash of something below, in the trees just off the trail, near where the three other mounted police were stationed. Just the play of sunlight on the leaves, he told himself, as he stared for a moment longer and nothing appeared. On the other side of the building, Weathers gave the command to take the cabin.

9—THE DRESS

The mounted policeman who had been conducting a lone pursuit of them these last days was quite fetching, Holly decided, as she urged her horse on down the trail. She had suspected as much when she first sighted him with her rifle at the Finnegan Ferry. It was part of what had led her to foul her aim that day. His smooth-shaven face—but for the thin moustache all the mounted police seemed to wear— and his hawklike visage, with those piercing dark eyes, it was all such a contrast to Morris.

She had been certain the constable was going to spot them both as they made their way down the hill to where the three sentries were posted. Somehow he had failed to, and when the men on the hill stormed the cabin, she and Morris had surprised the three men on the trail and stolen their horses. It had all worked out quite neatly, she had to admit, though when Morris had proposed it, she had thought it foolhardy in the extreme. And it would have been, she felt certain, if their pursuer had been below and not above. He would have been ready for their attack, been expecting it, unlike the three clueless lawmen they had set upon.

Now he was behind them again in pursuit, along with

the rest of the posse. She had not seen him, or any other riders, in the distance along the horizon, but she was certain they were there. They had done what they could to throw the law off the scent and put some distance between them—crossing and recrossing rivers and backtracking down streams—but Holly knew that any competent tracker would be able to pick up their trail again, and the constable had proven himself that.

They rode through the night until they had utterly exhausted the horses, hoping to gain a few hours on their pursuers. Their luck continued to hold, for as dawn broke the next morning, they came upon a ranch situated in a valley far from any other habitation. They stopped to study it before proceeding below and could see no one about in the yard. There was no smoke from the chimney, suggesting no one was yet up.

"Now listen, Holly dear," Morris said, his first words to her in some time. "We're doing things my way from now on, you understand?"

Holly nodded, though she was sorely tempted to point out that he had always insisted on doing things his way, so this did not represent a change in their partnership. She knew better than to do that, though, understanding that he was in a volatile mood, especially now, after an exhausting, sleepless night.

"You get to the barn and get us some horses saddled," he said, with a dismissive wave of his hand. "I'll see to whoever is in here."

Holly turned away and headed for the barn, not wanting Morris to see the disquiet she felt in that moment. Nothing good could come of this, her mind said, but she forced that thought aside. Just get the horses and be gone. The rest didn't matter.

The barn door groaned as she pulled it open, and she glanced back to see if it had alerted anyone in the house to their presence. Morris had already gone inside, and she peered through the dim light of the morning, the sun still behind the hills, as though she might discern what he was up to. Nothing was revealed to her, and she turned back to the barn and slipped into the darkness there, finding herself greeted by the familiar smells of hay, straw, piss, and shit.

A pig scrambled to its feet somewhere toward the back of the building, beyond where the shadows would let her see, eager for someone to feed it. There were three horses in stalls, and she found hay for them, while deciding which two to take. There was tack hanging on the walls, and, when she had made her choices, she started to saddle them. As she did, two shots echoed through the air, startling the horses, including the one she was in the middle of saddling, nearly resulting in her getting crushed against the side of the stall.

Holly did not linger after that, hurrying through the saddling and bringing the horses out of the barn. Morris was already on his way across the yard at a trot.

"What the damn hell took you so long?" he said, as she threw him a pair of reins.

"What happened in there?" she said, ignoring his question.

"Never you mind, never you mind," Morris said as they swung themselves up on their horses and started out of the valley at a trot.

Holly's disquiet returned, and she had to resist glancing back at the ranch house. What had he done?

It was only when they were out of the valley and well on their way that she looked over and saw the dress laid across the saddle between Morris's thighs. When he saw her glance, Morris smiled.

"Like I said, Holly dear. Things are going to change around here."

10—THE PUBLIC ROOM

It was a week before they picked up the trail again—a nearly intolerable week for Hestin, following along as Weathers careened about the territory with no conception of how to find the bandits, beyond simply stumbling across them. Hestin was left chafing under the strictures of the sergeant's command, desperate to set off on his own to find the traces he knew could be found, instead of following every gust of rumor to far the end of the winds, as Weathers seemed intent on doing.

They knew the two men had headed east out of the Cypress Hills the morning of the debacle at the trapper's cabin. Word had come a day or two later of a ranch house being stormed by two brigands, who stole two horses and some clothes. Fortunately, no one had been harmed. The ranch lay in a valley south and east of the hills, and Hestin had spent the following days saying to anyone who would listen that the two criminals were obviously heading south, hoping to get across the border before the NWMP could catch them.

And they would, Hestin thought, with some bitterness, because Weathers could seemingly not organize a simple search, though he could have called on all the manpower in the territory to support him. This he refused to do, no doubt because he was embarrassed by his utter failure in the Cypress Hills and did not want more witnesses to his incompetence, should it persist.

In the end, it was mere happenstance that they came across the bandits again. The police were passing through Lethbridge, the town near the old Fort Whoop-Up, on their way to Fort Macleod to resupply their force, when one of the constables overheard someone talking about a drunken man, dressed like he spent his days in the hills, spending money like a fool at the hotel. The constable brought the man to Weathers, who called on Hestin to question him.

The man—a farrier by trade—described the drunk to Hestin, who was quickly convinced that this was one of the bandits. He had long, tangled hair and an unkempt beard, both somewhat blond. The other man who had been traveling with him—younger and clean-shaven, but with long hair as well—was seemingly absent.

Now the bandit had taken up with a young woman. "A dox," in the words of the farrier.

"He's keeping her in fine style in the hotel. They never leave each other's sides. And they both travel with a pistol, I'm told."

Hestin relayed this to Weathers, who was charged with excitement. "By God, we've got the bastard now. He won't slip through our fingers again."

"It's strange the two men have split up," Hestin said. "I wonder what it means."

"Focus on the matter at hand, constable. We have one of the brigands now. He'll tell us what has become of his partner and we'll have the matter resolved."

Hestin bit back a retort, and the mounted policemen set about to work. They posted men on roads going out of town, in case the bandit attempted to flee before they were ready, while Weathers went to find the NWMP man posted there. Reluctantly, the sergeant had Hestin change from his uniform and wander to the west side of Lethbridge, where the hotel was, to confirm with the proprietor that the man and his woman were in their rooms.

Hestin strode into the small public room of the hotel, feeling self-conscious without his uniform. Eyes followed him as he made his way to the bar, where a vested man raised an eyebrow at him in question. Hestin ordered an ale and cast his eyes about the room. It was full of cowboys in town for the day, being entertained by harlots. All of them were watching Hestin closely, as though smelling an interloper in their territory.

Hestin kept his face steady and turned back to the proprietor, ready to ask him about the bandit and his woman. As he did, they appeared, walking down the stairs from the rooms above, the man unsteady on his feet, the woman watchful. The man went and sat at one of the tables where some of the cowboys were playing cards, pulling at his beard. He snarled at the woman to bring him a bottle of whiskey.

Hestin had to force himself to look away before the man noticed, but he had enough of a look to be certain it was one of the two men he had pursued. The woman came up to stand beside him at bar, asking in a cool voice for a bottle of whiskey. She gave Hestin a glance, and he felt her pause and stiffen, as though she recognized him. The proprietor handed her a bottle and she left, going to the table without a backward glance.

Hestin followed her movements, feeling certain that he had encountered her somewhere before, though he could not recall where. Something about her movements was familiar. Her face was not, though. She was plain-featured, with long, straight hair that had turned blonde under the sun. It was her eyes that drew his attention, though. They were green and flashed with vitality. He would not forget eyes like those.

The woman felt his gaze and turned to stare at him, her

face guarded. Hestin looked away, back to the proprietor. "Those two that just came in, at the card table there. The fellow looks familiar. They been here long?"

The proprietor grimaced. "Morris Danforth. Been here two days. He's been drinking the place dry and causing a ruckus. Seems no limit to their payroll."

"And the woman?"

"She arrived with him. I had her fixed for a harlot, but I don't think so now. She seems a decent enough sort. Don't know what led her to getting mixed up with his kind."

Hestin nodded and leaned across the bar. "Look, that fellow there is wanted for a robbery. Killed a couple people too. There's mounted police waiting outside town to arrest him."

"He don't leave this place," the proprietor said. "He'll be here all damn day, till he can't stand."

"Good, good. I'm going to head out and let them know where he is."

"He's got a pistol."

Hestin nodded. "Yes, I imagine he does. We're on the east end of town. You send word if he leaves or if he heads up to his room."

The proprietor said he would, sounding nervous. Hestin gave him an encouraging smile and finished his ale, turning to go. As he walked out, he glanced over at the table where the bandit was. The woman was watching him, her eyes intent. Why was she so familiar? The thought troubled him as he made his way back to where Weathers and the other mounted police awaited him.

11—LAST CHANCE

That the mounted policeman had not arrested them immediately, upon seeing them in the public house of the hotel, had surprised Holly. He had clearly recognized Morris and was trying hard to figure out where he might have seen her before. His mind would make the connection eventually, given enough time. Holly did not intend to give him the chance.

The problem was how to make her escape. Now was clearly the most opportune time to leave Morris to his fate. Especially since he had done her the favor of placing her in disguise. That the handsome constable had been out of uniform told her he was the advance man for a larger force awaiting them, probably outside of town. That force would be coming, now that the constable had confirmed Morris was present.

Holly's instinct was to run immediately. But running would be unwise, the more so because she was known throughout Lethbridge as Morris's woman. If she fled, the mounted police would certainly question her. If they arrested Morris, he would undoubtedly turn on her. She needed a way out that let her evade the authorities, while also ensuring that Morris did not.

It seemed as though the opportunity was going to be denied her, for Morris insisted on spending the afternoon at the table, gambling away the stolen payroll. Since their escape from the ambush in the Cypress Hills, he had grown increasingly belligerent, insisting that she never leave his sight, and that she wear the dress he had stolen from the ranch house. It was her penance for even thinking of betraying him, as he saw it.

"I let you be too free in your ways, Holly dear," he'd told her, "but now you got to be a proper woman and understand your place in things."

The dress was loose and ill-fitting, which was useful for Holly. She was able—during one of Morris's frequent blackouts from drink—to transfer the money she had sewn into her old clothes to her dress. The old clothes she had secreted, along with her pistol, in the hotel room, ready for when she did decide to take her leave. He had claimed her horse and rifle, but those were both tied to the crimes they had committed, and easily replaced with the money she had sequestered.

Now it was just a matter of getting out before Morris doomed them both. She grew increasingly anxious as the hours of the afternoon dragged on and Morris grew drunker and drunker, losing more and more of his dwindling stash. How long would the mounted police wait before they struck?

The shadows were growing long in the public room when Morris could no longer see straight and announced, to the few remaining patrons, that he was quitting for the day. To Holly's surprise, and the rest of the table gambling against him, he had made out well, increasing the stack of bills and coins he had brought with him. He went up the stairs, balancing himself equally between the railing and Holly, calling, in a voice heavily distorted by whiskey, for dinner to be sent to their room.

After dinner, he would fall into a stupor, from which he would not rise till morning. That would be Holly's last chance. She would have to be ready to seize it.

"Holly dear, Holly dear. You see how better things are now," Morris muttered as he fumbled for the key to their room. "You just listen to me and you see what I mean."

Holly did not reply, resisting the urge to help him in his search, having made that mistake the day before. She needed him docile and unsuspecting.

"I know what you're up to, girl. I know," Morris continued, as he extracted the key from his pocket and opened the door. Holly stood aside to let him lurch in to sit on the bed.

"You say this every day, Morris."

"Don't you tell me what I say. I know. I know. Damn you, Holly dear. I brought you here. Gave you all this money. This life. Not a bit of thanks."

"You know how I feel, Morris," Holly said, no longer paying attention. She went to the windows to look below and saw the streets filling with police, taking positions around the hotel.

"You can say nothing. I know. I know it, Holly girl. After all. After all. Damn you." Morris's voice grew louder.

Holly did not turn away from the window, scanning the faces until she found the man she was looking for. He stood beside a sergeant with another constable, looking contained and watchful, precise, as always, in his movements.

"Look at me, damn you," Morris shouted.

Holly mastered her conflicting emotions and pulled the drapes on the window closed. She turned back to Morris. "Rest awhile, dear," she said. "Supper will be up in a bit and I'll wake you."

12—HOLLY

Weathers led Hestin and another constable, Matthews, into the public room, where he met with the proprietor and confirmed the location of the bandit's room, while they ushered everyone from the place. Outside, the rest of the force stationed themselves around the building on the surrounding streets and stood ready, in the event Danforth made a break for it.

"He was drinking the whole afternoon. Could barely stand. His girl practically had to carry him up the stairs," the proprietor said, shaking his head in disgust.

"Good," Weathers said, his face flushed with confidence. "We've got the bastard for sure."

They cleared everyone from the rooms on the main floor as a precaution before heading upstairs, where the proprietor had assured them Danforth and the woman were the only people present. Weathers took the lead, the others trailing behind. He came to the door at the far end of the hall and knocked loudly, standing off to the side, away from any potential gunfire.

"Morris Danforth. This is the Northwest Mounted Police. Surrender yourself immediately."

Something between a grunt and a moan came from

within the room. Weathers glanced at Hestin and Matthews, and they all drew their revolvers.

"Danforth, the place is surrounded. There's no getting out. Come peaceably now."

A garbled reply followed, the only intelligible words: "Damn you."

"At least let the woman go, Danforth. She's no part of this." Weathers glanced at Hestin, sweat beading on his forehead.

Hestin opened his mouth to whisper something to Weathers, but he never had a chance to speak. Two shots from a pistol had them all diving for the floor. Silence followed, and the three men gradually stood, trying to assess the situation. None of them moved toward the door.

A woman's voice, quiet and timid, reached them. "I shot him," she said. "I shot him."

Hestin was the first to react, walking past Weathers to the door, which he found unlocked. He threw it open, entered the room, and saw Danforth sprawled out on the bed, his arms spread-eagled and his feet nearly touching the floor. The woman stood beside the bed in an odd pose, her hands clasped together before her, as though she didn't know what to do with them in the aftermath of her act. The gun, Hestin saw, was at the foot of the bed. He looked from it to the woman's face, which was unreadable.

Weathers pushed past him into the room, eager to take command of the situation. "Are you all right, ma'am?"

"Yes. I think so. Yes." The woman put a hand to her head as though she were faint.

"Best to sit down, ma'am," Weathers said in a solicitous tone, taking her by the hand and leading her to one of the chairs in the corner of the room. "Now, can you tell us what happened?"

"We were just waiting for supper to be brought up when we heard you outside. Morris got so angry, I was afraid of what he was going to do, and…"

"Take your time, dear," Weathers said, crouching beside her.

Hestin walked over to the bed and looked down at Morris. The man was dead beyond doubt, with two bullet wounds in his chest, right at his heart. A fine shot, he wanted to say, but did not. The woman, he noticed, was watching him closely.

"What is your name?" he said, as he bent down to pick up the pistol.

"Holly."

Weathers shot him a glance, which Hestin ignored. "And how do you know Mr. Danforth?"

"He's my husband."

"Did you know he was a wanted man?" Weathers said, putting a hand on Holly's. She did not so much as look in his direction, her eyes intent on Hestin.

"Morris was always one for trouble, in my experience. So I wouldn't be surprised at anything he got himself into. When he came back to me last week, flush with money, I knew he'd done something criminal. That was his way."

"He'd left you, then?" Hestin said.

"Yes. We settled in Montana, and he just up and took it into his head to head north. Wouldn't tell me why, but I knew it was one of his schemes. I decided I'd had enough and went back to my family in Taber. That's where he found me again."

Weathers nodded. "What did he tell you?"

"Nothing," Holly said with a shrug. "Said he'd money enough to set us up for a good long while. Wanted to take me back home again."

"So you went with him?" Hestin said. There was something about this woman that seemed very familiar and something about this story that didn't fit. Her expression, and the way she was watching him, like a cat observing its prey, made him doubt it.

"He's my husband," she said.

"Of course," Weathers said. "Of course. Why didn't

you head back to Montana?"

"We came here, and he got to gambling and drinking, and we never left. It's his way when he's got money. He never keeps it long."

"How'd he know you were in Taber?" Hestin said, ignoring another glare from Weathers.

"He just assumed it'd be so, I guess. I don't know. I always go there when he up and takes off."

"Hm. Now, can you tell us what happened?" Weathers said. "Take your time, dear."

"Like I was saying, we were waiting for supper," Holly said, choosing her words with care. "Then you yelled for him to surrender and it was like you woke a beast. He was wild. And I was so frightened. I didn't know what to do. He was saying he was going to shoot you, and going for his pistol. I just got it before he could. I don't really know what happened next."

She stopped, unable to say anymore. Weathers nodded in a consoling way. Her face was untroubled, though, and she was still watching Hestin for his reactions.

"Thank you, Holly. I think that will be all for now, yes," Weathers said. "Perhaps you should go and let us take the matter from here. No need for you to see any more of this."

Holly finally looked over at Weathers and nodded. The sergeant rose to his feet and gestured for Hestin to take her from the room. He offered the woman his arm. She took it, and he led her below to the public room. She sat at one of the tables, and he went to fetch her some water.

"Will I be in any trouble, do you think?" she said.

Hestin frowned. "That will be up to the judge, I imagine. Was anybody with Danforth when he came to see you in Taber? Or was there someone else with him when he first left?"

She shook her head. "Not in Taber. He was alone. He ran with all sorts of ruffians in Montana. Always has. He was a brute of a man. Such a brute."

Hestin wanted to ask her about the two shots she had taken—so precisely taken that even he was not sure he could have been as accurate under the pressure of the moment.

"You're a good man, constable, I can see. I'm glad that I'm in your hands." Holly looked up at him and smiled.

Hestin nodded uneasily, and the rest of their time together passed in silence. Weathers and Matthews came down the stairs fifteen minutes later, the sergeant solicitous toward young Holly as they led her out to the street. There Weathers conferred briefly with the constable from the Lethbridge detachment, leaving Hestin alone with the young woman again. He did not look at her, though he could feel her watchful eye upon him.

Finally, Weathers came over with the Lethbridge constable. "It's all been decided. If you'll just go with the constable here, Holly, he'll see to you."

Holly thanked the sergeant and Hestin, giving them both a cool smile, and let the constable lead her away. Hestin watched her, still feeling uncertain and unable to explain just why. He turned to Weathers to ask what he intended to do about the search for the missing bandit. From the corner of his eye he saw Holly look over her shoulder back at him. Her expression was hard to discern, but Hestin was certain he saw her smile.

13—MATTERS, SETTLED OR OTHERWISE

"The matter is settled, constable," Sergeant Weathers said, not bothering to hide his irritation. He pushed his hat back on his head and wiped the sweat from his brow with the back of his riding glove. "There's nothing more to say, and I don't want to hear it."

"We still haven't located any trace of the other bandit," Hestin said, persisting though he knew it would gain him nothing. His own forehead was damp with sweat, but he made no move to remove it, his eyes intent on the sergeant. It was a hot August day and the uniforms both men wore, heavy and woolen, did them no favors.

"He'll turn up, no doubt," Weathers said, waving a dismissive hand. "If he doesn't get picked up here for something, someone in Montana will do the work for us. Men like that don't stay clear of the law for long."

Hestin opened his mouth to argue further, but stopped himself. How could he put into words his suspicion that they already had the bandit at hand, that it was the woman, Holly Amos, who had been with him in the hotel room and had killed him before they could arrest him, without sounding like an utter madman? There was no possible way, for he had no evidence. Only a hunch, based on nothing more than his impression from their few conversations together, that the Amos woman was hiding something.

"And best to put this woman from your mind," Weathers continued, oblivious of Hestin's conflict. "Oh, you do have to wonder a little about someone that would agree to a marriage with the likes of Morris Danforth. But she's young and she'll have a chance now to make better decisions going forward. The judge doesn't hold her culpable, and I can't say I disagree."

"She knows more than she's telling us, sir," Hestin said quietly, knowing this was the kind of thing that had resulted in his banishment to the Wayne dispatch.

"Maybe so, maybe so. A wife knows a lot about her husband's doings, maybe even more than he suspects. That doesn't make her guilty of his crimes, now does it? No, the matter is settled. Unequivocally. I'm going to get on my horse and head back to Fort Empress. I suggest you get on yours and get to Wayne. Your lieutenant will be waiting for you."

With that, Weathers saluted, Hestin responding in kind automatically, and stalked away to join his men, muttering to them about the damnable heat. There were only three remaining in Lethbridge, the rest having been sent back to Fort Empress with the manhunt concluded. The sergeant climbed atop his horse, followed by the other men, and with a final salute to the constable, they rode out the gates of Fort Whoop-Up, heading east.

Hestin watched them go, before turning away, nodding to himself, and went to find his own horse. He followed the others out of the gate, but instead of going north to return to Wayne, he went south toward Lethbridge. The matter might be settled for Weathers and the judge, but it was not for Hestin. He intended to seek out the woman Amos and see if he could put the doubts in his mind to rest.

14—A PARTING

Holly shifted in her seat, trying and failing to find a comfortable position for her dress. Though it was loose-fitting, and though she had worn it these last weeks, it still did not feel right to her. She had been too long wearing breeches and shirts to find the strictures of a dress comfortable, and she was counting the days until she could shed this costume for her regular clothes.

Those she still had, for they had been among the things in the hotel room. The mounted policemen had looked them over, but failed to notice they were too small for Morris to wear. When they were through investigating, and when the trial was over, she had claimed them, along with her rifle and revolver, and Morris's pistol, giving the Mounties some sob story. She needed the guns to sell to get a little money, now that they had confiscated the stolen payroll cash, and the clothes she wanted as something to remember Morris by.

Her portion of the stolen payroll remained hidden in her dress. She had not touched it in the days following the raid on the hotel, crying poverty and relying on the kindness of the mounted police and the townsfolk to carry her through. They considered her a poor, put-upon wife of a no-good scoundrel, but before they had thought her nothing more than a whore, so she considered they were only getting what they deserved, more or less.

She looked up from the table where she sat, the tea in her cup growing cold, to look about the public room of the hotel. It was still early, so it was quiet, with only the proprietor and a few other guests having breakfast sharing the room with her. The gambling tables were empty and the harlots were still asleep. The peace was, Holly decided, disconcerting, though it did allow time for contemplation. That went against her better inclination, though.

As far as where her next steps would take her, Holly had not thought that far. She still did not entirely trust that she was going to escape justice in the matter of Morris's killing. It all seemed too good to be true. Until they let her ride away, she would not believe it.

Given how often she had pondered leaving Morris and striking out on her own, she had few ideas on what to do now that she was afforded the opportunity. She had money, but not enough to live on indefinitely, though certainly she could manage to stretch her dollars farther than that drunkard Morris. Soon enough, though, the cash would be gone and she would be back to where she always began, broke and needing another score.

It was a life, she supposed, though not an easy one. And the law would be watching her, now that they knew she had killed a man. No matter that they had said she was innocent, they would not forget that. Every mounted policeman in the territory would know her name. It would make things more difficult, especially her thieving. She would have to take care.

The more she thought about it, the more Holly came to realize that being free of Morris had not freed her of all her shackles. She had just exchanged them for some new ones. But that was always the way of things, she supposed. This time, at least, she would not tie herself to a drunken fool who refused to listen to sense when it was spoken by a woman.

As the thought occurred to her, she looked up and saw Constable Hestin enter the public room. There was something about his powerful shoulders and sharp eyes, his perfectly trimmed moustache and spotless uniform, that stirred welcome feelings in her. His eyes cast around the room and found hers and, in spite of her worries about avoiding the law, she gave him a beckoning smile.

He approached her, his expression serious, and, at a gesture from her, took off his gloves before pulling out a chair to sit opposite her. Holly studied him with what she hoped was a demure gaze that disguised the hunger of her curiosity. This man was not like the other policemen she had come across. He was capable and deliberate, which made him dangerous. And alluring. For he was so different from Morris, with his debauchery and his wild swings of emotion.

"Constable, I'm surprised to still see you in town," she said, giving him another welcoming smile.

His serious expression did not change. "I leave for Wayne today. Before I do, I wanted to see you."

"Is that so?" Holly said. "What an honor. To what do I owe it?"

Hestin looked away, as if he was unsure how to proceed. "What will you do now that you're free to go? Head back to Taber?"

Holly shook her head. "I was just pondering that myself. I don't know, to tell the truth. I don't think I will go back to Taber. There's nothing for me there."

"Surely there's your husband's land?"

"Sadly no," Holly said, but did not elaborate, hoping her pained expression was enough to stall any further questions along those lines.

"I see," he said, frowning. "Well, I'm sure you have family you can go back to."

Holly gave what she hoped was an enigmatic shrug. Hestin pursed his lips. He was watching her very carefully,

Holly noted, and she wondered why. Far too clever, this one.

"I wanted to ask you again about your husband's friends. Is there anyone else you can remember him spending time with? We still need to find whoever was working with Danforth. They're responsible for two murders."

Holly was careful to keep her expression neutral and her eyes upon the constable's. An easy task, for they were eyes she enjoyed studying. "I've already told you all the people I can remember Morris bringing around. Like I said, most of his viler friends were from Montana. I didn't see much of them at all."

"Of course," Hestin said, still watchful. "If I could entreat you to write me at the Wayne dispatch if you recall anything else, I would be much obliged."

"It would be my pleasure, constable."

Hestin hesitated, unsure of himself. Why, Holly wondered, was that the case? He was not a man to suffer from doubt.

"Well, ma'am, I should be on my way," he said, pushing back his chair and standing up abruptly. "Good luck in your journeys, wherever they may take you. Perhaps we'll see each other again someday."

"Perhaps we will, constable," Holly said, with a nod and a smile.

As she watched him go, she thought it would be foolish in the extreme to ever allow herself to come in contact with Constable Hestin again. He was far too clever and far too honest. He would see through her eventually.

And yet, as the constable disappeared out the door, she found herself wanting to follow him back to Wayne. It was a mining town, with all that meant, and not even two years old. There would be easy money there for the taking, both honest and dishonest, for someone like her who knew what she was doing. It was as good a place as any in this territory to sit and stay for a spell. Which was an attractive thought, with all the running and privations she had suffered through with Morris.

There was the constable to think about, though. As she did, Holly found herself smiling, and the matter seemed almost settled.

PART TWO

15—OLD ACQUAINTANCES MET

The Last Chance Saloon was the sort of establishment that more than earned its name. Filled with miners after their shift, harlots, gamblers, cardsharps, thieves, and worse, it was the sort of place Holly knew well from her days traveling with Morris. She gravitated to it soon after she arrived in Wayne and found herself a room at the Rose Hotel just down the street.

The hotel was poorly named, or perhaps just ironically so, for there was nothing attractive about it. Like the rest of Wayne, it had been built in a hurry following the opening of the mine two years prior and the influx of people to the new town that had come with it. Before there had been only a few ranchers and homesteaders scattered about the badlands and the river valley and now even the towns nearby were starting to fill with people eager to make see their fortunes made. The town smelled of sawdust and new lumber, among other, less appealing scents, and the homes and buildings were all plain as a result. On the edges of town they were downright ramshackle, little more than shacks thrown together with whatever spare lumber lay at hand.

But Holly did not dwell too much upon the attractiveness of the town, for its surroundings more than made up for what the habitation lacked. The Red Deer

River valley provided spectacular vistas, especially as seen from parts of the town, which sat about halfway up the river valley, surrounded by the strange hills of the badlands, with their tops covered by long prairie grass and their sides bare of any vegetation. There were furrows running down the sides where the runoff from snow and rain went, twisting and curving their way down along its auburn-colored face to the river and its many tributaries.

The only thing Holly had found to dislike about the river valley was that it was unconscionably hot, even now as they came to the end of September. The bugs were fearsome as well, the mosquitos relentless in their harassment. If they dissipated, it seemed horse flies or hornets or some other variety of pest would appear. But she was used to such tribulations from the months she and Morris had spent out on the plains, whether in this territory or Montana, and she could manage them well enough here. When they were gone, it meant winter had come, and that was its own struggle.

Holly had arrived in town the day before, but had mostly stayed to her rooms. Now that she had made her way to the Last Chance, she was unsure of her decision to come. The impetuousness of it all seemed foolhardy to her suddenly, which it certainly was. There was no purpose to her being here, beyond a vague feeling that she wanted to stay near Constable Hestin. This, in spite of the danger he posed to her. He suspected her of being involved in the payroll job with Morris and the kinds of work she would find here in Wayne would only confirm these suspicions. No, there was only trouble to be found in towns like Wayne, but perhaps it was trouble she was looking for.

As yet, she had no prospects to make money, and while she still had a nice supply of cash remaining from the payroll heist, that would not last long here. Despite its rather spartan accommodations, the Rose Hotel was expensive to stay in—the town having grown so quickly that there were not enough beds available for those who wanted them. Yet Holly wasn't worried; she remained confident that circumstances would provide her with opportunities soon enough.

And the Last Chance was the place that would provide it, she felt certain. Her confidence was rewarded before she had even finished her first beer. A familiar face came stumbling down the stairs from harlots' rooms above, a disheveled grin upon his face. Holly watched him through narrow eyes, following him as he made his way to the bar in fits and starts.

As he leaned against the counter and made his order, Holly sidled up alongside him. "Harold Morton," she said, still surveying the rest of the bar.

"Who wants to know?" Harold glanced over at her, failed to recognize her, and looked her over again. "What's a pretty thing like you doing dressed like that and in a place like this? Looking for a man to take care of you?"

Holly turned to meet his eyes. "I got tired of that a while ago, Harold. I'm looking for something else."

"Are you sure? I can take good care of you. Keep you right satisfied."

"I doubt you can satisfy yourself right now," Holly said.

"You got a damn foul mouth on you, girl," Harold said. "I'm of a mind to set you straight."

"You can try if you want. But I know for a fact I can shoot straighter than you. At fifty yards. Or a hundred."

Harold flushed with anger, readying an angry retort, before realization washed over his face. "Holly Amos, I'll be damned. Didn't recognize you without your man. I heard he got himself killed."

"That he did," Holly said.

"I hear he knocked over the Atlas payroll. A messy business. Surprised you didn't get mixed up in it too?" Harold peered at her closely with unsteady eyes.

"He and I had gone our separate ways before all that."

"That so?"

"It is," Holly said, then finished off her beer and waved at the bartender for another.

"So what brings a sure shot like you to Wayne, then?" Harold said.

Holly held out her hands. "I'm open to suggestion."

Harold nodded. "Might be I can think of a few things. Might be."

"I'd be interested to hear them," Holly said. "I'm at the Rose Hotel."

Harold gave her a smile and lurched away, weaving through the crowd to one of the faro tables. Holly watched him go with narrowed eyes. He would be in touch, she knew. A scoundrel like Harold was always into something, or would know others who were. For the first time since she had entered the Last Chance she felt at ease.

It was still light out when she left the Last Chance, though the sun was steadily dropping behind the hills, bringing out the red in the badland rocks. Holly set off down the street toward the Rose Hotel, whistling to herself and feeling very satisfied with her day. As she passed the town general store, Clive Hestin stepped out from its door and into the street.

"Miss Amos," he said, looking her up and down with a quizzical eye.

"You can call me Holly, constable," she said, smiling warmly at him.

"What brings you to Wayne, Miss Amos?"

"Oh, I just couldn't bear to go back to Taber and pick up that old life. That unfortunate business with Morris seemed like a good opportunity to start fresh somewhere else."

"So you came here," Hestin said, doubt plain in his voice.

"That's right," Holly said, feeling her face flush. She had not prepared herself for this meeting, though she should not have been surprised to encounter him on the street. He was the law here, and though the town was booming, it was not overly large, with no more than a thousand souls present.

"What are your plans, now that you're here?"

Holly shrugged. "Oh, I expect I'll stay for a bit and see if I like it. If I do, I might see about setting something up."

Hestin seemed about to question her further about her presence in town, but thought better of it, evidently. Instead, he asked where she was staying.

"Presently I am at the Rose."

"Not expecting to stay there long, Miss Amos?"

"Holly," she said, with a firm smile. "I expect to take things as they come for now, constable."

"Indeed," he said with a nod. "I'm surprised to see you dressed so."

Holly looked down at her clothes. She had bought new pants and a shirt, along with a coat and hat, in Lethbridge. They were men's clothes, but unlike what she had worn during her time with Morris, these did nothing to disguise the fact she was a woman. She was grateful she had left behind her revolver and holster in the hotel room; they would have only brought more questions from the constable. Though she supposed those would come soon enough.

"Oh, I much prefer these to a dress," she said. "With Morris gone, I had to do so much of the work. It's much easier to get your hands dirty in these sorts of clothes."

Hestin studied her closely. "I imagine it is, Miss Amos, I imagine it is."

He tipped his hat at her and started down the street toward the Last Chance. Holly turned and watched him go, her mind filled with doubts. Her first encounter with the constable on his home turf had not gone at all as she had imagined. Perhaps it had been a mistake coming here after all. She was taking a great risk, and it was not at all clear what she had to gain.

16—THE HANGED MAN

In spite of all the problems Clive Hestin had to deal with, he could not stop thinking about Holly Amos. There was something about her presence in Wayne, so soon after the murder of her husband, that bothered him, though he couldn't put his finger on why. The two were unrelated, in all likelihood. And yet...

Holly did not seem at all broken up about the death of her husband. Not that Hestin could blame her for that. Morris Danforth was, by all accounts, a ruffian of the first degree, and the territory was better off with him gone. But someone like Holly Amos, who had spent her days eking out an existence on some piece of land near Taber, waiting and perhaps fearing those days when Danforth would return, did not seem the sort of person to up and go to Wayne, where she had no prospects and knew no one.

Unless, as he had long suspected, the image Holly had presented at the trial was not a true one. The fact that she was so apparently unaffected by her act of killing gave Hestin pause. Even if her feelings for Morris had soured, there had been something there once. And it wasn't as though she were used to killing. Or was she?

Hestin had watched her from the general store as she

sauntered down the street, a commanding and self-possessed presence, so different from the demure figure she had been in Lethbridge. It was not simply the clothes, he told himself. There was more to it than that. She seemed alive now, in a way she hadn't before, the light he had caught glimpses of in her eyes cascading outward to encompass her entire being. A strange transfiguration.

But Hestin did not have time to ponder the mysteries of the Amos woman. That matter was closed, unless Danforth's compatriot was foolish enough to reemerge. And there were pressing issues that needed attending to.

First among these was the problem of Gene Archibald, the proprietor of the Last Chance Saloon. If there were criminal things happening in Wayne, Archibald was likely to be at the center of them, or knew who was. If there was a rigged card game, a protection racket, general intimidation of landholders, or suspicious death, then the first person to talk to was the proprietor of the saloon.

Yet, in spite of the fact that Hestin had arrested dozens of men with links to Archibald, there was little to tie the proprietor to any of the crimes. Certainly, none of the men he arrested were talking. It was, if the man himself was to be believed, all a matter of coincidence.

"I can't control who comes through these doors, constable," Archibald had said on more than one occasion. "And I can't control what they talk about, or who with. And I certainly can't control what they get themselves up to afterwards."

Hestin wasn't so sure that was the case. But Archibald was careful not to involve himself too directly in anything. And when there was a slip-up and something or someone seemed to implicate the proprietor in whatever malfeasance was afoot, he, or his most trusted compatriots, moved very quickly to make sure that the evidence disappeared and people fell silent.

Which brought Hestin to his second problem: his superior officer, Lieutenant Cavanaugh. A man Hestin had assumed was a lazy drunk, whose general incompetence led to any number of people escaping punishment for the crimes they had committed, but who was not actively malicious. That impression was now called into doubt by the events of the past day.

The morning before, Hestin had been called to the Atlas Coal Mine, where Gerald Yates, a ruffian of no account, was being held in the overseer's office. He had been caught waiting south of the mine, on the road back into town, to rob the miners who had just been paid their weekly wages. It was an old scam—a tried and true one that Hestin found himself dealing with every few months, and he thought nothing of it.

The evidence was clear, and there could be no doubt as to what had occurred. There were the two men who Yates had attempted to rob, and two others who happened upon them while the act was in progress, to swear to that. Not that it mattered; Yates as much as admitted to the crime when Hestin came to bring him back to town.

He had left the man in jail, under watch of Lieutenant Cavanagh, while he went about the rest of his day's work, not giving the incident another thought. When he returned to the detachment that evening, it was to discover Yates dead, hanging from a rope in his cell. He sprinted across the main room of the detachment to the back where the two cells were. He cut the rope and let the body down, but it was too late. Yates was dead.

Hestin felt the body after he lowered it to the ground. It was already going cold and stiff, which meant the man had hanged himself hours before, while Cavanaugh had somehow remained oblivious. The lieutenant was in the front room of the detachment, in clear sight of Yates' cell, and presumably had been there all day and should have seen what happened. But he was sound asleep in his chair, and no doubt had spent much of the afternoon asleep or drinking, paying no mind at all to the man in the cell.

Trembling with rage, Hestin left the cell and went over

to the chair where the lieutenant slept, legs propped up on small writing desk that might as well have been a footstool, for all the writing Cavanaugh did on it. Before he could bring his emotions under control and stop himself, Hestin kicked the chair in which Cavanaugh sat, knocking it over and sending the man toppling to the floor.

Cavanaugh sat up with a start, looking around wildly to see what had caused his fall. When he saw Hestin looming over him, his eyes went dark with a murderous rage. "What in God's name do you think you're doing, constable? I'll write you up for a reprimand."

Hestin's hands were shaking, he was so furious. He knew he should be stopping himself—Cavanaugh was his superior officer after all, and no one in the force would take his side. Not after what he had done in Fort Macleod. But he didn't care. The man had simply gone too far in the dereliction of his duty this time. And it had cost a man his life.

"Go ahead, lieutenant. I'll do the same. I'll tell the superintendent that you let a man in your care hang himself because you were too drunk to stay awake to keep a watch on his cell."

Cavanaugh blinked in surprise, though Hestin was not sure whether he was taken aback by his anger, or at the fact Yates had died under his watch. The lieutenant's eyes narrowed and he took a step toward Hestin. "Is that so?" he said, his voice wavering from drink. "You do that, constable. You do that. But be sure that you explain how you left a man alone in his cell with a length of rope to hang himself with."

It was Hestin's turn to be surprised. In his fury following the discovery of the body, it had not occurred to him to wonder at where the rope had come from. He had searched Yates when he picked him up from the Atlas overseer's office, but it had been quick and perfunctory, to ensure the man had no guns on him. Even still, he was certain there was no way Yates could have possessed a length of rope as long as the one he had used without it being discovered.

"I did nothing of the sort," Hestin said, a sinking feeling taking hold in his stomach.

"Well, he must have had it with him to be able to hang himself. He couldn't very well have walked out and gotten it. I wish you good luck in explaining it. I'm sure the superintendent will believe you."

The sinking feeling became a pit as Hestin saw what would happen with a sudden clarity. No matter what happened now, if he wrote a letter or did not, he would be made to take the blame for Yates' death. Cavanaugh would see to that.

"Yes, I can just imagine how the superintendent will receive such a letter," the lieutenant said. "How will you explain it, I wonder? Will you say he had it hidden on his person? Or did someone bring him a bit of rope? He couldn't very well have gotten by me, I can tell you that."

Hestin thought it likely that the entire police force and a tribe of Blackfeet could pass through the detachment without Cavanaugh noticing when he had been at his drink, but he did not say so. One the lieutenant's questions sparked a thought in his mind. "Did anyone come to see Yates today?"

Cavanaugh was taken aback by the question. He spluttered. "I just said someone couldn't get by without my noticing."

"I know, lieutenant. I'm asking if anyone came to see him today."

"Of course not. That's ridiculous. Who knows the man in town? I've never laid eyes upon him until today."

"Nor have I," Hestin said. *That doesn't mean someone else hasn't*, he thought. "Did anyone come by today, lieutenant?"

"No," Cavanaugh said, his voice gruff and his eyes downcast. He looked, if Hestin could put a word to it, fearful.

"Gene Archibald wasn't here, was he?" A stab in the dark, but one that the constable could see struck home. There was naked fear in Cavanaugh's face now, as well as desperation.

"I don't what the hell you're talking about, Hestin. But you best not try anything with me. The superintendent still listens to me, even if you won't."

Hestin did not reply. He gave the lieutenant a small, knowing smile, turned on his heel, and left the detachment. His anger returned, coursing through him. Cavanaugh was not simply derelict in his duty; it appeared he had aided Gene Archibald in a murder. Hestin marched toward the Last Chance Saloon, intent on confronting Archibald and letting him know that at least one mounted police in Wayne would work to uphold the law.

It was as he was on his way to the saloon that he saw Holly Amos, dressed like a cattle hand, exit it and start toward him. Before he could think, he ducked into the general store, intending to let her pass, though he could not have said why he was concerned about seeing her now. The moment of doubt and confusion passed, and by the time she reached the store, he decided he needed to find out what she was doing in Wayne.

When their conversation was over, he did not continue on to the Last Chance. His doubt about everything had returned. Had he seen fear in Cavanaugh at the mention of Gene Archibald, or had he just wanted to? Was he trying to avoid the possibility of his own responsibility in the matter for having failed to notice the rope?

But there had been no rope, of that he was certain. Everything else was at question and remained to be determined.

He decided to return to the detachment and deal with the body. Certainly Cavanaugh wouldn't. Archibald could wait until morning. But as Hestin had the mortician called for to deal with the body and looked over the cell, finding nothing, his mind kept returning to Holly Amos. Even as he sat down to write a report that would go to the superintendent, which he started half a dozen times, trying to find the words that would implicate Cavanaugh without doing so directly, his mind turned to her.

That he saw her leaving Archibald's place on the same day as the Yates murder was likely coincidence. And yet... He could not forget the two perfectly placed shots in Morris Danforth's heart, or the payroll man who had been shot through the eye. There were far too many questions now, and he had no answers. His first step, he realized, was to discover just who Gerald Yates was.

17—GENE ARCHIBALD

Harold Morton called on Holly at the Rose Hotel early the next morning following their meeting at the Last Chance. He looked as though he had spent the rest of the day and the better part of the evening carousing and now was the worse for it. His eyes were bloodshot and heavy, his voice barely more than a rasp, and a stray beam of sunlight was enough to make him wince.

"You look like got ate and spit out because you didn't taste too good," Holly said by way of greeting as she waved him into her room where she was finishing the last of her breakfast.

"You always had a tongue on you, girl," Morris said.

Holly shrugged. "How can I help you?"

"The boss wants to see you."

"Who might that be?" Holly said.

"Gene Archibald. He owns the Last Chance. If something happens in this town, he gives his say so, you understand? He's got some work for you."

Holly made a face. "I don't work for folks, Harold. If I wanted to do that, I would have stayed on the homestead."

"That may be so," Harold said. "But if you want to do any work in this town, you need to talk to Gene. You

64

don't want to cross him. I've seen what happens to those that do."

Holly nodded, thoughtful, as she looked at Harold. He had always struck her as someone looking for a boss to follow. She was not that way. "So this Archibald, you work for him?"

"I do work for him," Harold said proudly. "And I help make sure everyone follows the rules while in Wayne, if you understand me, Holly."

"Is that so, Harold?" Holly said with a smile.

"It is so," Harold said gravely.

"What's this Archibald like?"

"You'd best see that for yourself."

"Well, then," Holly said, and drank up the last of her coffee. "Let's go see him, shall we?"

The Last Chance Saloon had only a scattering of miners just starting into their cups as Harold led Holly through the main room to the back. She caught glimpses of young women in slips, and smelled coffee, eggs, and beans. As they passed down a narrow hallway, the soft voices became hard and gruff and they came to a closed door.

Harold held up a hand to knock upon it just as someone within shouted, "You're telling me I can't be making a living in this town? You got no damn right and you know it. I got that money fair and square."

The next voice they heard was lower, projecting a calm iciness that reached them through the door. "You got that money because I let you. Don't forget it. Now, if you don't like the way things work here, it's a free territory and you can head on out. But I think we both know there's plenty of money to be shared around here. Wouldn't you agree?"

There was a reply, but it was quiet and defeated. Harold looked at Holly, raising an eyebrow, as though to say, *I told you so.* He knocked upon the door.

"Come on in, Harold," the calm and quiet man said.

Harold opened the door and waved Holly in. She stepped in and saw two men sitting across from each other. The first, with his back to the door, was a large man with a heavy mustache and long, tangled hair that went around the crown of his head, which was bare. Though he was the larger of the two in the room, his shoulders were hunched over and he peered up as though the other man was looming above him.

The quiet man, who Holly assumed was Gene Archibald, was clean-shaven, with dark hair that he combed back and a thin mustache that he had obviously waxed and trimmed as precisely as his hair. He had a slight build and small hands that did not look as though they did much work, but his stare was fierce; it seemed to possess Holly as he followed her entrance into the room. She found it difficult to breathe, until he looked over at the man seated across from him.

"Thomas, I believe we were done," he said, with the same quiet menace.

Thomas stood reluctantly, not glancing at Holly or Harold. "I got to eat, you understand. You can't just be taking money from me and mine. I got kids and a wife."

"What I'm proposing is more than fair. It's no different than what anyone else is getting here. You pay the same as them. Now, I have other matters to attend to."

Thomas looked as though he wanted to argue more, but Harold was at his side, taking him by the arm. He looked from Harold to Gene, nodded in surrender, and turned to go. Harold followed behind him, closing the door as he left. Gene Archibald watched until the door was shut and then turned his attention back to Holly.

He stood up from his chair and gestured for her to sit, not returning to his seat until she had. "So, you are the sure shot. Holly Amos," he said, leaning forward and putting his elbows on the table, pressing his fingers into a steeple beneath his chin.

"That I am," Holly said. "You must Gene Archibald.

Harold has a lot to say about you."

"Harold is a good man. He vouched for you, which counts for a lot with me."

"So what can I do for you?"

"Right to the point, are we? Well, I understand you're a good shot. I have need of a good shot."

Holly raised an eyebrow. "That so? I don't kill people for money, if that's what you're looking for."

Archibald smiled. "Harold tells me you ran with Morris Danforth for a time. He wasn't above some killing if there was money to be made, from what I've heard."

"That's a different thing entirely."

"There's a degree or two of difference, I suppose," Archibald said. "At any rate, I don't need you to kill someone. That's not the kind of game I run. I just need someone who can kill someone if it becomes necessary. If you understand me."

"Let's say I do," Holly said. "What kind of game am I getting myself involved in?"

"Well, Harold probably told you that every racket in this country is under my watch. Everybody pays their piece if they want to go ahead with it. That's the arrangement. But, as you just saw, not everyone is pleased with that. Some of them get a bit more rambunctious than old Thomas. I have a couple of boys like Harold who don't mind mucking it up, but none of them is much use with a gun."

"Harold could be if he ever saw straight enough to shoot," Holly said.

Archibald laughed. "That's true, no doubt. At any rate, it's one thing to be willing to bring your fists to bear on a situation and it's another to put a bullet in a man and know he's not getting back up. From what Harold tells me, you're the second kind of person."

Holly studied the man across from her, considering her reply. He was entirely too pleased with himself, too sure of his authority. And she also did not believe for a second that he wouldn't send her off to kill someone if he saw some benefit in it. He was not the sort of person who kept a hired gun and then didn't use them. But then, who was?

"Let's say I am," she said. "What's in it for me?"

"All business, then. That's what I like," Archibald said. "Let me put it this way. Any game in town has to run through me, so any two-bit scam you might run, you have to give me mine. You work for me, you get a part of the whole."

"I'm not one to stay put in one place, so I'd be sacrificing quite a bit if I took up with you. You're gonna make it worth me while."

Archibald looked at her with a smile. "I'll make it worth your while."

18—MORTIMER MCCAULEY

Hestin was up and on the road to the Atlas Coal Mine before dawn. There he stopped each miner that passed to ask whether they had seen Gerald Yates before. Only the men who had been involved in the robbery could recall him. The overseer, when Hestin stopped in at the mine to check, said the same thing. It seemed as though the man had just arrived in town—if one could call lurking on the road to the mine being in town—which led to the question of why someone would want him dead.

Hestin was about to leave to return to Wayne and continue with his investigation when he asked the overseer if Mortimer McCauley was at the mine.

The overseer nodded. "He's been here since yesterday. Been up before daylight, I expect."

The overseer pointed in the direction of a large house sitting further up the hill from the mine entrance and the overseer's offices. Hestin trudged up the narrow path, wondering why McCauley would bother with building a house so near the mine. It wasn't as though he was here often. He spent most of his time in Calgary, where he had a large ranch, coming up to Wayne only when circumstances demanded, given it was two days' hard ride.

A young man with a reserved expression, wearing a well-tailored suit, opened the door before Hestin even had the opportunity to knock. "Constable," he said, taking in Hestin's uniform. "Please come in. How may I assist you?"

"Thank you. I'm wondering if I might speak with Mr. McCauley."

"Of course," the young man said, inclining his head. "What is your inquiry about, if I can be so bold?"

"I arrested a man yesterday who was robbing the miners of their pay just down the road. I found him dead later that day in his cell. And now I'm trying to find out who might have known him."

The young man raised an eyebrow. "Surely you don't think Mr. McCauley was familiar with a common thief?"

"I don't think anything. I'm just here to follow any lead."

"This man's death was suspicious?"

"That is part of the investigation," Hestin said, watching the young man closely.

He looked decidedly unimpressed by Hestin's explanation. "I'm afraid Mr. McCauley does not have time for idle inquiries."

"I understand, but it will only take a moment—" Hestin began.

As he spoke, the door behind the young man sprang open and McCauley thrust his head out the door. "Borders, what are you doing? We don't have time to waste."

A pained expression crossed Borders' face, which disappeared by the time he turned around to face the mine owner. "This constable—forgive me, I didn't get your name—has come to inquire if we know anything about a thief who was evidently assaulting the miners."

McCauley frowned, stepping through the door and coming to shake Hestin's hand. "Mortimer McCauley. How many I help you, constable?"

He was, Hestin guessed, in his late fifties, his fine head

of hair gone silver and his middle beginning to go soft, but he still moved with the vitality of a younger man. His grip was firm and hard, the hand of a man who had spent a life working, which stood in stark contrast to the fine grey suit he wore. He was, Hestin noted, wearing riding boots, a small concession to life in a frontier town.

"I won't take up much of your time," Hestin said. "Yesterday I arrested a man who was stealing the pay from your miners on the road to Wayne. He died while in our custody and the matter is under investigation. I'm trying to see if anyone at the mine knew him."

McCauley shook his head. "This is the first I'm hearing of this," he said. He turned to Borders. "Were you aware of this?"

Borders shook his head, wincing slightly.

"This is a great concern of mine. I need my workers to be safe. I can't have ruffians on the road doing this. The roads seem to be getting worse. Our payroll was hit last month, as I'm sure you know."

"Yes, I found the men."

"Terrible thing," McCauley said, with a shake of his head. "But you got the man. Or at least his wife did."

Hestin nodded.

"This is just a damnable problem. We can't be having our payroll stolen. I've doubled the number of men on the payroll, but all the same. We need that railroad built. It's damned expensive to be shipping coal by wagon still, but at least no one wants to steal it. When we started mining, we expected the railroad to be built within the year. But this bloody government—they don't care about what happens in the territories unless there's an uprising."

Hestin nodded sympathetically. "It would be a great help to the town as well."

"Yes. Exactly. Now this fellow was caught, you say? And murdered?"

"He was found hanged in his cell. The circumstances raise some questions."

"I should say," McCauley said. "Though I can't say I'm sorry. The bastard got his. What was this fellow's name?"

"Gerald Yates."

McCauley took a step back in surprise before recovering himself. "Yates, you say? Never heard of him. Borders?" His assistant shook his head, and McCauley shrugged. "Sorry we can't be of more assistance, constable. But do let me know if there's anything we can do to help."

He shook Hestin's hand a second time and was out of the room before Hestin could thank him. Borders looked at him, and Hestin took the hint and left the house, heading back down the hill toward the mine and his horse, his head filled with thoughts about Gerald Yates, a drifter of no account who apparently knew one of the wealthiest men in the territories.

19—DAYS FILLED

Holly took well to working for Gene Archibald, in spite of her misgivings about the man and the job. It was easy work, at least for now. Every scoundrel in the country knew not to cross the proprietor of the Last Chance and made sure to pay their respects and more regularly. It was the first steady pay Holly had ever had—ten dollars a week, and more if the week was a good one—more than enough to keep her room at the Rose Hotel. In fact, she was able to move into a better one upstairs and add to her stash from the payroll job.

Archibald clearly liked having her at his side when he went about town. Soon everyone in Wayne knew who she was, in part thanks to the stories he and Harold spread. She was the wife and partner of Morris Danforth, the killer and thief who had stolen the Atlas payroll and led half the mounted police in the territory on a merry chase. More than a wife, she was a capable gun in her own right.

Word had still not reached Wayne about the circumstances surrounding Morris's death. The constable was obviously not talking, though why he wasn't, Holly couldn't say for certain. When it did, and it certainly would, the stories told about her would change. And so would Harold's friendliness toward her, she supposed. But that was a problem for later.

For now, she collected Archibald's money and stood at his side when he wanted to be particularly threatening—not that he needed much help in that regard. His business interests extended beyond Wayne to encompass several nearby hamlets, including Rosedale and East Coulee, and even as far east as Dorothy. He had piece of every saloon in those places, and there wasn't a game of faro or poker that took place without him getting a cut. And that did not include all the petty grifting, whoring, and whiskey trading he had a part in.

"Just you wait till the railroad finally gets here," Gene said to her, when she remarked on the extent of his business. "This town'll explode. The mine will expand and the miners will be looking for what they're always looking. Liquor, women, and cards. And I'll make sure they can get them. Just stick with me, Holly, and you can be a part of all that."

He told her that more than once, and each time she would simply nod and smile. She had no intention of being a part of that, for she had seen enough of Archibald to know what that would entail. A part of meant he owned her, same as he owned the women in the Last Chance. Holly had no interest in being a gun in someone else's holster.

For now, she would stay. The pay was good, after all, and her days had to be filled. And there were other things to keep her interest in Wayne. But that too would eventually wane, and when it did, she would be on the first horse out of town.

20—OTHER MATTERS

The matter of Gerald Yates remained unsolved, at least to Constable Hestin's satisfaction. Lieutenant Cavanaugh had sent on his report that said otherwise, and heavily implied Hestin had been derelict in his duty. Nothing had come of that yet, and Hestin doubted anything would. It would be something to hold over him when the opportunity arose— not that the superintendent had any issues in that regard.

Though he still had many questions on the matter, Hestin had reluctantly set them aside. No one, aside from Mortimer McCauley, knew Yates, or if they did, they were not speaking on the matter. He had sent word to all the forts and detachments in the territory, and none had any record on the man. If Yates was a drifter, he had not drifted many places nearby.

He turned his attention to other matters, and there were no shortage of those in a place like Wayne. Not with men like Gene Archibald around to cause trouble and escape all blame. The woman Holly Amos was running with him now, which piqued Hestin's interest, and there were stories that she had run with Morris Danforth, as well as being his wife. None of them squared at all with the tale she had told in court of a quiet life spent in Taber, and it led Hestin to wonder again if she had been involved in the payroll job.

When he asked Harold Morton about it one day, while doing one of his periodic run-throughs at the Last Chance, the man denied it. "Oh no, they'd gone their separate ways by then. Apparently, she was in Taber, looking after her mother, when all that mess went down."

Hestin wasn't sure he believed that at all, but he had no evidence one way or the other, so he let it lie. Partly that was because he was reluctant to confront Holly again. There was something about her that left him ill at ease. She lied with alacrity, but he had known many men who had done the same. Just as he had known many men who could handle themselves in any situation, as she seemed to. But he had never known a woman like Holly Amos.

21—A CONVERSATION OVERHEARD

Holly and Harold arrived back at the Last Chance just as dawn was creeping over the badland hills. They had been down the road to East Coulee to talk with the man who was running a faro game out of a shack there and had decided he should be an independent operator. A little chat from Harold and some glowering from Holly while she fingered her holster were all that was required to convince the gentleman that he was better off paying his dues to Archibald.

There were still a couple of miners seeing the night out at one of the card tables in the main room, but all the girls had gone to bed and Stephen the barman looked asleep on his feet. He started when Harold slapped the bar counter and asked for two whiskeys.

"Gene was looking for you," he said to Holly.

She nodded. "Save mine for now," she said, and went to Archibald's office.

The back of the saloon was quiet and Archibald's door was shut. She leaned her head against it to see if anyone was in there with him. She had made the mistake of walking in on him up to his hips in the skirt of one of his girls, a mistake she did not intend to repeat. The look he had given her, the beckoning smile curving his lips, had both attracted and repelled her.

Gene was saying something in his even voice that she could not make out, and it was followed immediately by a voice she did not recognize. "You said you would handle the damn Yates thing."

"I did," Archibald said.

"If making a hash of it is handling it, then I guess you did."

"He's dead, isn't he? He's not telling anyone anything now."

Archibald sounded impressed with his argument, but the other man was decidedly not. "Yes, but the damn mounted police was up at the mine asking questions about the whole thing. Now the whole country knows about Yates. And he sent letters to every fort and detachment in the territory. If somebody puts two and two together…"

"Nobody will," Archibald said. "You worry too damn much."

"I don't worry when I know a job has been done right. That's what we pay for. If you're not going to manage that, then I don't know why we're in business together."

"You want the job done, but you don't want to get your hands dirty. That means you got no say in how it gets done. If you want to get down in the muck with me, you're free to do so. And then you can tell me how you'd like things done."

There was an air of threat in Archibald's voice, and the other man did not reply. Sensing their conversation was drawing to a close, and not wanting to be caught standing outside the door when the other man left, Holly knocked and called out, "You wanted to see me, boss?"

There was a pause on the other side of the door and then chairs began to scrape as the two men stood. "Come on in, Holly," Archibald said, and she opened the door.

And was met by the glaring face of a handsome young man in the finest tailored suit Holly had ever seen. He looked as though he felt dirty just standing in the office. Turning back to face Archibald, he said, "Just see there are no more foul-ups. And remember the schedule."

He stalked from the room, giving Holly a final, chilling stare, slamming the door behind him as he went. Archibald gave the door a mocking wave goodbye before gesturing to Holly to sit down.

"Who was that?" Holly said.

"Don't worry about him. He's all saddle, no horse."

Holly nodded, though she wasn't so sure that Archibald was right. There had been a violence in the other man's stare that had unsettled her.

"Everything go all right tonight?"

Holly nodded, her thoughts still on the young man.

"Good. I have another job for you. We're going to see how good of a shot you actually are."

22—A SILENT CONFRONTATION

The sound of the river reached Holly's ears from where she crouched under the shadows of the trees that lined its banks and stretched up into the broader valley. The earth was damp from rain that had fallen the day before, and the air was crisp with the hint of the autumn that was soon arriving. From where she lay, rifle nestled in her arms, she could see the road below, where it forked to head down the river and the narrow bridge there.

She shifted slightly to relieve a cramp in her elbow, sighing and muttering as she did. It was bad enough to be here and doing this; the waiting made it insufferable.

As she thought about how interminable the wait had been, she heard a horse approaching on the road and had to hurry to ready her rifle to shoot. This was not at all what she wanted to be doing, but she had known this was inevitable from the moment she had agreed to work for Gene Archibald. The money had been too good, and she had not gotten restless and left soon enough. Doing so now would only encourage him to send men after her.

She set the rifle against her shoulder, balancing its length upon her outstretched arm, and brought her finger near the trigger as she put her eye to the sight. There was little breeze and the road was not far away, so it promised to be an easy shot, but she took nothing for granted, slowing her breathing. And she waited, listening to the hooves upon the road.

The rider paused at the fork before turning right and heading down toward the river and the bridge that lead into Rosedale. Holly held her breath and set her finger on the trigger, ready to fire. She took her hand away as soon as the rider became visible, still holding her breath and not daring to move otherwise. It was the constable, in his distinctive scarlet Norfolk jacket and pillbox cap, tilted on the right side of his head.

What was he doing here?

It did not matter—so long as he kept on the road into town, he would not interrupt her task. But the constable did not. He pulled his horse to a halt and looked around as though he had heard something. His gaze came to a rest on the copse of trees that Holly was hiding in, disturbing her greatly, though she told herself he couldn't spot her from the road. She had checked herself earlier. But she could not shake the feeling that he could see her, and had to fight the urge to slink away.

At last, the constable turned back to the road, apparently satisfied, and urged his horse on. Holly sighed in relief and closed her eyes, though she did not truly relax until the hoofbeats disappeared. That, she told herself, had been entirely too near a thing.

Just as she began to recover, she heard more horses approaching, along with the wheels of a wagon, and readied her rife again. The wagon turned at the fork and came into sight, pulled by two horses. Holly could see Horace Goodstone sitting on the narrow seat with reins in his hands, and at his side was his young daughter. The girl said something and her father leaned down to better hear her over the clatter of the horses' hooves and the grinding of the wagon wheels on the road.

Holly swore under her breath, taking her hand away

from the trigger again. Damn Archibald. This was not at all what she wanted to get mixed up in. But she was and there was no escaping it. If she didn't act now, she would miss her chance and there would be hell to pay later. She drew a deep breath and held it, bringing Goodstone into her sights, and squeezed the trigger.

The scream of the shot echoed through the river valley, a sound that always gave Holly pleasure. Her aim was true, which satisfied her more in this instance. The bullet hit Goodstone's hat dead center, passing through it, and it landed somewhere on the other side of the road. He instinctively ducked, certain he had been hit, and threw himself on top of his daughter to shelter her in the event there were further shots.

The horses were startled and leapt forward, nearly pulling the reins from his hand. When Holly saw that he still had them, she let off another shot behind the wagon, but close enough that it would seem like a near thing. The horses pulled the careening wagon out of her field of vision, and soon she heard them clattering across the bridge. Goodstone would get them under control soon enough, and if not, there would be plenty of folks to aid him in Rosedale.

When she could no longer hear the wagon, she got up from her hiding spot and made her way back along the river half a mile or so, where it turned out of view of the road and the bridge, and where she had tied her horse up. It was still there, placidly chewing at the grass, and nickered at her approach.

She made her up through the trees to the road, letting the horse finds its own path through the tangle of brush. They came to the road just west of the fork and where she had hidden herself earlier. Though she knew she should not linger here now, doubt gnawed at her and she rode toward the fork, pausing where the constable had paused, and peered into the depths of the trees.

As she stared into the shadows, trying to confirm to

herself that the ground where she had lain was obscured, the constable stepped out from the trees a little south from her hiding spot. He did not appear surprised to see her. His gaze went from her to her saddle, where she kept her rifle tucked away. Holly drew her breath in sharply and fought the urge to turn her horse and gallop away.

The constable took a step forward, watching her very closely, his hand straying to the revolver at his side. He opened his mouth to say something but stopped and did not take another step forward. Their eyes locked on each other's, neither of them speaking, Holly's horse dancing in impatience the only movement between them.

A meadowlark trilled its distinctive song somewhere down near the river, and both of them turned toward it in surprise. When their gazes returned, whatever spell had held them earlier was broken. The constable took a halfhearted step forward, stopped again, and watched as Holly turned her horse and headed down the road.

23—A PROBLEMATIC KISS

"Sure shot, huh? That's some pretty shooting, no doubt. But you didn't do the job I sent you for. Now explain that."

Archibald was visibly angry, which Holly had never seen before, though he had not raised his voice at all. They were in his office at day's end, the bustling chatter of the saloon's main room, punctuated by the odd loud shout or hysterical laugh, reaching them. Archibald's eyes did not stray from hers, his whole being intent upon her, not allowing for any interruptions.

"It sends the same message," Holly said. She had stopped in East Coulee on her return to Wayne, spending the better part of the afternoon in one of the bars there, getting the courage for this confrontation.

"Do you think so? I don't pay you to think. I pay you to use that gun of yours. If you're not going to do that, what good are you to me?"

"It sends the same message," Holly said again. "And without having the mounted police getting too excited."

Archibald shook his head. "You don't know our fine constable very well, do you? It's true, the lieutenant is as useless as tits on a boar. But that constable is trouble. He'll get his teeth into something like this and he won't let go."

"But if I'd killed Goodstone, he would have had something to get his teeth into. This way, if they somehow figure out it was me, I can just say I was hunting prairie chicken. There's no way to prove otherwise."

Archibald stood and walked around his desk to loom over her. In spite of his slight build, he was an intimidating presence. He leaned down so that his eyes were level with hers and his breath was upon her lips.

"This will cause a lot of problems for me. If you'd done what I said and the constable got snoopy, we could have got you out of the territory without too much trouble. Now, he knows to be on his guard and he knows where to look, and I haven't done what I said I'd do."

Holly swallowed, her mouth dry. She gripped the armrests on the chair to stop her hands from shaking. There was no telling what Archibald would do now. Men like him were unpredictable. Or all too predictable, especially in moments like this.

At last, a trace of smile crossed Archibald's lips. "It's just a good thing for you I like you, Holly Amos," he said.

He pressed his lips against hers. They were soft and sweet, and he smelled slightly of some perfume that Holly found intoxicating. Her heart raced with excitement at the kiss, even as the rest of her sagged with relief that she had managed to escape his wrath. At least for the moment.

Archibald straightened and turned away. "Now get out of here."

Holly stood, feeling dazed, and a little angry at herself for the desire she felt. She resisted the urge to touch her lips. "You don't have anything you want me to do, boss?"

He turned back to look at her, taking her all in. "Not for the moment. Not for the moment."

"What about this problem?" she said, regretting it immediately. He had given her an opportunity to leave and she hadn't taken it. She wanted to stay, even if she didn't like the way he was looking at her just then.

"Leave that to me for now. And the next time I tell you to shoot someone, sure shot, you shoot them."

Holly nodded and left the office before Archibald could change his mind. Or before she let herself do something she knew she'd regret.

24—AT TWILIGHT

Constable Hestin returned to the detachment at twilight, the air turning cold. There might be frost tonight, and for that he was glad he had picked the tomatoes from the little plot he kept behind the building. The detachment was empty, Cavanaugh having wandered off somewhere in a drunken stupor, and neither of the cells filled.

Their emptiness seemed a mockery of him, so he turned his back on them. Instead he went to the shelf beside the lieutenant's desk and pulled the few books out until he found the bottle Cavanaugh always kept hidden there. He sat down in the lieutenant's chair and took a long pull, wincing at the bitterness of the liquor. Cavanaugh must have gotten it from one of the whiskey traders, because it tasted as though it had been cut with kerosene.

Hestin stared morosely at the beams that crisscrossed the ceiling, trying and failing not to think about that afternoon. The dereliction of his duty. He was no better than Cavanaugh. He had let the Amos woman leave without so much as word or a raised hand, when he knew beyond any doubt she was the one who had taken the shot at Horace Goodstone.

The worst of it was, he could not say why he had done

so. She could have killed the man, but had not—he had seen Goodstone's hat for proof of that. But he had not looked at that until after the he had let her go. All he knew for sure was that she had tried, for reasons that remained unclear, to kill Goodstone. Having seen the hat, he now felt certain that she had been with Morris Danforth on their mad dash across the territory. She had killed at least one of those payroll boys, had nearly shot him at the ferry—though perhaps that miss had been deliberate as well—and finished it all up by killing Danforth.

Now she was in with Archibald, and apparently was taking shots at local farmers for him. It was one thing when Archibald's little schemes inflicted their hurt on other gamblers and thieves, or took money from men who should know better. This was something else entirely, and it needed answering if there was to be anything approaching law in Wayne. It was baffling to Hestin that Archibald had done something so bold, so certain to draw a response, even from Cavanaugh.

Holly might have some answers as to why. But he had let her go.

He took another slug of the lieutenant's terrible whiskey. What was it about this woman that left him feeling so unsettled and led to him forsaking his duty and everything he believed in? It was madness, was what it was. There was no one else who could inspire that in him. And thank God for that, he thought, taking another swig.

Hestin stayed in the lieutenant's chair for an hour or more, slowly drinking his way through the bottle of whiskey, his thoughts growing steadily more morose. He had failed utterly as a lawman, it was clear. Alienated his fellow officers by refusing to turn a blind eye, and what had it gained him? He was just as compromised as they were, only he had done it over a woman he'd barely spoken to.

He tried to tell himself he had done some good here for people in this territory, but he wasn't sure that was the case. The peace had been kept in Wayne and in Fort Macleod, but little more. Crime flourished and men mostly did as they wanted to. The affair with Morris Danforth seemed emblematic of his career. He had chased the man across the entire country but been unable to bring him to justice. The woman who killed him had gone free and continued to mock him with her presence in this town and in his thoughts.

It was dark, both outside and within the detachment, by the time he stirred from the chair and returned the bottle to its hiding place. He fumbled at the desk for a match to light one of the lamps, thinking as he did so how strange it was that Cavanaugh had not returned yet. Normally he did not stray from the detachment when he was at his drink, preferring the comforts of his chair and bed.

As Hestin dug a match from the box, he heard something. A footstep upon board or a leg clipping against a wall. It sounded as though it had been outside, but very near. He went still, hand poised with the match, listening intently, but heard nothing else. Glancing around, he saw only shadows. Shaking his head, he bent over the lantern, turning it toward him and raising his hand to spark the match with his thumbnail.

A blow struck him on the head as the match sparked to life. It tumbled from his hand, its light dying, as Hestin pitched forward, tangling with the chair and landing so hard that the air was knocked from him. The shadows seemed to move, and a dark boot emerged from them and struck his head. All he saw after that were colors and darkness swirling together as the whole world shifted beneath him.

He smelled kerosene from the lamp all around him and a new light, focused and sharp, emerged from the darkness above him. It descended to the floor and began to spread all around.

PART THREE

25—JEREMIAH JAMES

Holly wanted nothing more than to return to her room in the Rose Hotel and go to sleep. Her meeting with Archibald had been unsettling for any number of reasons, and after an afternoon of drinking, she was in no particular shape to sort out her thoughts on the man. All she knew for certain was that he would not hesitate to have her kill or kill her if he thought it was necessary.

She passed back through the saloon, struggling to navigate the crowd. It was a busy night—with the miners' pay having come in, they were availing themselves of all that the Last Chance offered. More than one drunken man, mistaking her for one of the girls from upstairs, made a grab for her, but Holly deftly sidestepped them on her way to the door. Only one miner managed to get a hand on her, and she made certain he regretted the choice.

She was still enjoying his cries of pain when a familiar face stepped in front of her. Jeremiah James had run with Morris for years before he took up with her. Even after, they would sometimes work on jobs together. Holly had never much cared for Jeremiah, partly because he brought out the worst in Morris. Inevitably, after a job, the two of them would abscond with the money and spend it all on liquor. When Morris returned to her after a day or two, he would be domineering and ugly, just like Jeremiah always was.

Jeremiah held up a large hand when he saw her, which she made to brush past. He didn't let her, taking hold of her arm and pulling her toward him. Jeremiah was a towering man of fearsome strength, and he squeezed her arm hard, making her wince. He did not look pleased to see her.

"Holly Amos," he said, in an accusing tone.

"Jeremiah," she said. "Let me go. I'll see that you regret it."

"Is that so?"

Holly nodded. With her free hand, she pulled a knife from her belt and thrust its point toward his groin. Jeremiah leapt back, releasing her as he did so.

"I forgot that you don't fool around, Holly," he said, sneering.

"No, I don't," she said. "Especially not with fools like you." She turned to go.

Jeremiah called after her, "We have unfinished business to see to, Holly Amos."

Reluctantly, she turned around. "What would that be? I have seen you in months and I don't owe you a damn cent. In fact, you probably owe me."

Jeremiah took a menacing step forward. "I heard what you did to Morris."

Holly was careful to keep her face steady. "Is that so? What tale were you told?"

"Weren't no tale, Holly. I heard it from a mounted police himself. You shot Morris with his own damn gun. And then played the innocent after. Oh, he was some surprised when I told him you'd rode with Morris for years. Some surprised. Said you was wearing a dress, playing at being a wife. You ain't no wife, Holly Amos."

Holly forced a smile to her lips, slipping her knife back into her belt, though she kept her fingers on its handle.

"You're gonna believe some lawman over me?"

"I am," Jeremiah said. "I always told Morris he should never have trusted you. Well, he was damn fool enough to and paid the price. But if the law ain't gonna see you answer for it, I sure as hell will."

"That so?" Holly said, and Jeremiah nodded. She looked at him, trying to judge how drunk he was. He seemed in control of his faculties, but she knew there was no chance he was actually sober. "How do you propose to do that?"

"You talk big, Holly. You talk big. But we both know that's all it is."

She opened her mouth to reply, but was interrupted by Harold, who stumbled between them, a vague smile on his face.

"Well, I'll be. Jeremiah James. What brings you to Wayne?"

Jeremiah did not take his eyes from Holly. "I got some business to attend to."

"That right?" Harold clapped him on the back. "You should talk to Gene Archibald. He's the man to talk if you want to do business here. Me and Holly work for him."

"Is that right?" Jeremiah looked down at Harold.

"Damn straight. He's a good man, Gene is. Always looking for a fellow like you who can handle himself, if you know what I mean."

"I'll have to have a talk with him. Once my business is settled."

Harold nodded eagerly. "Absolutely. Holly or I can have chat with him. He'd be glad to have you on."

Jeremiah looked from Holly to Harold, a thin smile on his face. "Strange that you'd be working with her."

Harold looked at him blankly. "Why's that?"

"You haven't heard what happened to Morris?"

"Yeah, he knocked off the payroll here and got himself shot up in Lethbridge."

"Do you know who did the shooting?"

Harold shrugged. "The law."

Jeremiah shook his head and looked at Holly. "It was her."

Harold stared at her as well, uncomprehending. "No," he said. "She wasn't with him then. They split before the job."

"It's true, Jeremiah," Holly said. She wanted to run from this unfolding disaster, but forced herself to stand and face it. Running would only serve to confirm his claims.

Jeremiah laughed. "Harold, you don't believe her, do you?"

Harold turned from one to the other, looking confused. "Sure," he said. "Why the hell would she kill Morris?"

"The law was onto them. It was her only way out. She killed him. Probably took the payroll with her."

"If that were true, why would I be here working some two-bit job for a saloon owner?" Holly said.

Harold looked slightly offended, but nodded. "She's right, Jeremiah. We're not making fortunes here. Not yet, anyway."

For the first time, something like doubt crossed Jeremiah's face. It was there for a moment and then vanished. "I don't believe it."

"You're so full of it," Holly said, sensing an advantage. "I didn't kill Morris. I didn't have anything to do with that payroll job. That you'd trust a lawman over me or Harold tells me all I need to know about you, Jeremiah. You never liked me, not from the start. I was the one that took Morris away from you."

Jeremiah gritted his teeth, his face going red. "What the hell are you saying?"

"You know damn well what I'm saying." Holly allowed the slightest of smiles to cross her lips.

Jeremiah's face went a deeper red and he began to holler over the clamor of the bar. "You take that back.

94

You goddamn whore. You take that back."

He started toward her, but Harold stepped in between them and held him back. Holly made sure to stand her ground.

"The whores are upstairs," she said. "But you wouldn't know where to find them, would you?"

"You goddamn... You goddamn... I'll see you pay for what you did. Don't you doubt it. This ain't over."

Jeremiah continued to shout at Holly, even as he let Harold lead him away to the bar. Harold glanced at Holly and gave her an enigmatic shrug. She watched them go, exhaling and taking her hand from the knife at her belt. A near miss. But as Jeremiah had said, the matter was far from over.

She turned to go, to return to her room, collect her thoughts, and determine what she should do now. As she did, she caught a glimpse of the lieutenant from the detachment emerging from one of the rooms upstairs, hanging off one of Archibald's girls. She looked twice to make certain, for he was not wearing his jacket, but there could be no doubt it was him. It seemed odd that he would let himself be seen there, but then, he was a drunk, as everyone knew.

That oddity, as well as her problems with Jeremiah and Archibald, disappeared from her mind as she started down the street toward the Rose Hotel in the cool of the night. The town was on fire.

26—RESCUE

The smoke was the first thing Hestin noticed as consciousness slowly returned to him. It was everywhere. It was in his lungs, and it felt as though he was drowning. He started coughing and couldn't stop. Each ragged breath he drew only brought in more smoke and ash. He opened his eyes and saw flames and darkness.

This is the end, he thought, and was paralyzed.

The loud crack of a beam above him, sounding as though it was near to falling, startled him from his terrible reverie. He pushed himself up, his vision swimming as he did so. The flames were very near, all around him. It seemed a miracle he had not been consumed yet, the fire dancing near his feet blackening the cuffs of his pants.

He got to his knees, glancing about through the fog of the smoke, trying to determine where he was in the detachment and, more importantly, where the door was. If he chose wrong and ended up in the back by the cells, he was likely finished. Tears ran down his face and his throat ached from the smoke as he tried to find some landmark through the darkness and haze that would let him know where he was.

It seemed to be getting hotter by the moment, and

sweat mingled with his tears. He would not last much longer. He had to act now or perish. Rising into a crouch, he started forward, reaching out to try to find a desk or something to orient him. He was still suffering from the effects of the blows to his head, and they, along with the smoke and flames, left him utterly disoriented and fumbling.

After a few steps, he toppled to the floor, surrendering to a spasm of coughing that seemed as though it would never subside. The flames seemed to come nearer and nearer, licking at his flesh, leaving scalding marks. He tried to rise again, but it felt as though he had swallowed flames. He fell back to the floor, lay there, and closed his eyes to wait for the end.

Somewhere he heard the sound of glass shattering. The whole building seemed to groan and rage. The flames seemed to be shouting at him, hectoring him.

"Constable. Constable," they said. "Damn you."

I am already damned, he wanted to say, but his lungs were ash and his tongue was fire.

Hands grasped his shoulders, and he fought against them, thinking it was fire itself come alive to seize him.

"Damn you," it cried.

It was no good: the hands had him and he began to move. The flames crept closer, the smoke billowing around. He could not stop coughing. He felt himself raised up and at last felt a breath of sweet, cool air reach his cheek, and he gasped in delight. Coughing followed, but in what remained of his mind, a dim thought came. It was the window. If he could get out...

He tried to move toward it, pushing against the hands, and fell hard upon the floor.

"Damn you," the fire said. "Do you want to burn or what?"

I do not, he tried to say, but the coughing would not allow him.

The hands seized him, and he felt himself rising again.

Before he realized what was happening, he was tumbling down and landing on the ground. It smelled of earth, of life. The hands took him again, dragging him away, and he opened his eyes. Above him, he could see the stars and the moon.

The rest of the evening for Hestin passed by in a series of distorted and unconnected images that only later he was able to put any meaning to. His rescuer had dragged him out one of the windows alongside the detachment, the entrance having been consumed by flames, and then pulled him into the middle of the street, where he was left to recover. As he lay there, coughing and wheezing, a fire brigade was started—or perhaps it had already begun— and the flames were slowly quenched.

It was hours until they were extinguished entirely, and it seemed the whole town gathered to help out. Even the miners, drunk and disorderly from the Last Chance Saloon, pitched in. Someone summoned Doc Evans and, with the help of a few others, he brought Hestin to his place to recover. The doctor put liniments on the burns on Hestin's hands and legs, wrapped them in bandages, and mixed up a tincture to help with his cough. There must have been some opium as well, for Hestin fell into a deep and painless sleep.

When he awoke, it was still dark out. No sounds reached him. A hush seemed to have settled over the town, which he presumed meant that the fire had been doused. He shifted a bit on the doctor's bed, but the pain from his burns told him that was inadvisable. Though he was exhausted and everything seemed to ache, his thoughts raced of their own accord and would not allow him to return to sleep.

He tried to piece together what had happened. All he could recall before his rescue was sitting and drinking the lieutenant's whiskey in the detachment. Someone had struck him on the head and started the fire, but the memory of that was hazy. As was all that followed, a series of pictures that he could not put in any coherent order. There were two things he was certain of. He had not seen Lieutenant Cavanaugh amongst the crowd of the fire brigade before Doc Evans took him away. And though he had only seen her face briefly after she had dragged him from the building before she vanished into the night, he was certain his rescuer was Holly Amos.

27—THE MORNING AFTER

The talk in the Rose Hotel public room over breakfast was all about the fire the night before. Holly sat by herself in a corner and listened. Ann Galvert, the wife of the proprietor, who was always about in the mornings, told Holly that the constable had been inside the building when it caught but had somehow escaped.

"He says someone hit him in the head and knocked him out and started the fire. Can you believe it?" Ann said, shaking her head.

Holly just shook her head as well, stunned by the terrible ways of the world.

"But he's all right at least, thank God. The detachment's ruined, though."

Holly nodded, and Ann drifted on to the next table, hoping for a more receptive audience. Holly watched her go, feeling a sense of relief, though she couldn't have said why. Her efforts to save the constable's life were apparently unknown. It shouldn't matter if the whole town knew, and yet Holly felt somehow that it would. Perhaps it was just her unease following the night before, when she had been faced with threats from both Gene Archibald and Jeremiah James, men she knew were more than capable of following through on them. But then, so was she.

And what did it matter that she had saved the constable? It was of no consequence to anyone. Yet she could stop thinking about Archibald's last words to her, promising to take care of the problem. He didn't intend to kill Goodstone—at least, Holly didn't think so. If he still wanted that done, he would have demanded that she do it. Had he meant that he was going to kill the constable? Had the fire been set by him?

She couldn't quite believe it. Why take the risk of bringing the entire mounted police force into Wayne? For that was what would happen if one of their own died. Unless it had been intended to look like an accident—and the man in charge of the detachment had reported as much to his superiors. Lieutenant Cavanaugh had been at the Last Chance the night before. It had seemed merely strange before, but now the memory took on a sinister hue in her mind.

Why had he been there? Had he been told to make himself absent? Or was he simply a drunk doing as a drunk would?

When she finished her breakfast, she pushed these questions aside. There were more pressing matters at hand, and she had avoided them for long enough. Archibald would be waiting for her at the Last Chance, as would Jeremiah. Her instinct was to get on her horse, ride in the opposite direction, and wait for the tempest to blow over. Or never return. That might be the smartest choice left for her here.

Instead, she drained her cup of coffee and then strode out of the hotel and down the street to the Last Chance.

Harold shook his head at her when she walked into the public room. He was standing behind the bar nursing a glass of lager, spitting tobacco into a spittoon between sips. His regular breakfast, then.

"He's in a right mood this morning," he said, wiping the dark spit from his lip. "Don't know what happened, but he's something angry."

Holly wandered up to the bar and let Harold pour her a lager. "What happened after I left?"

Harold shrugged. "Well, I got Jeremiah calmed down and took him in to talk with Gene. They had a head to head for a while. Then word came of the fire at the mounted police detachment and everybody headed out to help out."

"Quite the scene," Holly said.

"Sure as hell was. Didn't see you there, though." It was an accusation.

"I was there when the fire was first spotted. Helped out a bit and then made myself scarce when the rest of the town showed up. That lawman is always watching me. Didn't want him getting ideas I started the fire."

Harold nodded. "He was in there, you know. Somebody dragged him out. Saved his life. Would have spared us a lot of trouble if he'd gone up smoke with the rest of the building."

Holly shrugged and took a pull on her beer. "I don't know. His lieutenant's still here, ain't he? And the mounted police will just send someone else along. Maybe someone worse."

"We don't need to worry about the lieutenant. Gene's handled that. And nobody could be worse than Hestin. The man is a lawman through and through."

Holly opened her mouth to ask about how Archibald had managed to take care of the lieutenant, though she suspected she knew the answer. Before she could ask, Archibald emerged from his office, his face ugly with anger and his eyes pooled with shadows of exhaustion.

"Where on God's green earth have you been?" he said when he spotted Holly.

She was careful not to betray any emotion. "At the hotel, eating breakfast, like I do every other day."

"Don't get smart with me, sure shot. I've had enough of it. You've caused me trouble enough already, girl."

Holly stopped herself from replying. She recognized this mood from Morris. Gene was dangerous right now, filled with a fury that needed to find some outlet. She would have to take care that she was not the one on the receiving end.

"Come on, then," Archibald said. "We've got problems to deal with now, before things get totally out of control."

Holly started after him as he walked toward the door, followed a half-second later by Harold. Archibald stopped and shook his head. "You stay here. Cavanaugh will be coming by this morning, I'm sure, and he'll be a blubbering mess. Do whatever you have to to keep him together. Get him drunk, get him a girl. Whatever. You understand?"

Harold nodded. "Sure thing."

Archibald went out, blinking at the sunlight, and got on his horse, Holly a step behind. Together they rode out of town down the road to the Atlas Coal Mine.

28—CONSEQUENCES

Instead of heading directly to the mine, Archibald led Holly off the road onto a winding path that made its way through the surrounding hills and up above the mine. They emerged atop the hills overlooking the entire river valley. Behind them was a vast stretch of prairie, as endless as the sky. Below, Holly could see a footpath that led to a house situated above the mine.

Archibald looked at Holly, climbed off his horse, and hobbled it, then started down the path. Holly did the same and followed behind. They continued below to the house, scrambling along the path, neither of them speaking, though Holly was filled with questions and trepidations. Against her better judgment, she had left her rifle on her saddle, reasoning that if Archibald wanted her to bring it, he would have said so.

Carrying on without it left her feeling exposed, but she did not see that she had any choice. It would not matter anyway. If someone from the house wanted to kill them, they could do so now easily. Archibald did not seem concerned, his eyes intent on the house, and soon enough, they had descended and were crossing over to where the house stood perched atop another rise.

It was, Holly realized, the largest house she had ever seen, by quite a large margin. She could not imagine who might be living here in the middle of nowhere near a mine. Anyone wealthy enough to build such a place, could surely afford to put it somewhere nicer.

They were just stepping up onto the broad veranda when someone came out the door to confront them. It was the same handsome young man she had overheard meeting with Archibald before. Here, in his element, he looked even more beautiful, his fine suit not standing out, as opposed to at the Last Chance. The violence simmering within his dark eyes was still present and still left her unsettled.

"What are you doing here, Archibald? And why are you bringing your thugs with you?" the man said.

Archibald smiled, apparently at ease and feeling in command of the situation. "We have a problem."

"You're supposed to be solving my problems. But you seem to be unqualified to manage that. You're quite good at creating more, though."

Archibald's expression did not change. "The thing with Goodstone was done like you asked. Holly here took a couple of shots at him, nearly killed him. Put the fear of God into him, I've no doubt, Borders."

"If Goodstone could be frightened, I think he would have been by now, don't you? We had agreed, I thought, that he was to be killed, as a message to the other landowners that it would be in their best interests to move along."

Archibald glanced at Holly, as if to say, *I told you so*, before turning back to Borders. "We'll see how it plays out. But that's how it was done. Keeps the law from getting too interested, anyway."

Borders smirked. "I fail to see how that would be the case with the constable still about. I assume you, or one of your very capable lieutenants, were responsible for last night's fiasco."

Archibald shrugged. "Who's to say who started the fire? Could've been anyone, really. It's unfortunate someone helped out the constable. But we still have Cavanaugh to handle that situation."

"All Cavanaugh can handle is a bottle of whiskey. You're just lucky none of this Hestin's superiors give a damn about him, or we'd be drowning in mounted police."

"Well, they don't. And I can still get Cavanaugh to play our tune."

Borders shook with anger and had to visibly control himself from lashing out. "So tell me, Gene: unless you've come here to recount for me all the ways in which you've failed me, I cannot fathom why you would put me and Mr. McCauley at risk of being associated with a criminal of your ilk by coming here with your pretty little hired gun. Why the hell are you here?"

Archibald looked from Holly to Borders and back again. "I know things have gone a little bit sideways here. But it can all still be put to rights again. That's what I came to tell you, to promise you and Mr. McCauley that he can put his mind at ease. As a gesture of goodwill and to show that I intend to set things right, I've brought you one of the thieves that knocked over your payroll."

Holly was so taken aback by Archibald's words that she was unable to do more than stare at him. Anger came a moment later, but by then Archibald had drawn his pistol and pointed it at her.

"I had a chat with Jeremiah James last night. He had a lot of interesting things to say about you, Holly Amos."

It was Borders' turn to look from one face to the other. When his eyes lit upon Holly's, she had to resist a shudder. A cold sweat formed beneath her hat and on the back of her neck.

"Is what you say true, Archibald?"

"She ran with Morris Danforth, and before he ran with

her, he was with this James fellow. He swore to me there was no way he would have done a job without one of them. He wasn't a good enough shot to take out your men from that distance in the canyon. Holly here surely is."

The smallest of smiles touched Borders' lips. "If she's such a good shot, why are you willing to let her go?"

Archibald smiled as well, and Holly felt very cold. "Well, like I said, consider it a gesture of goodwill. I know how much that payroll raid hurt what Mr. McCauley's trying to do here. And I've got a replacement for her. Maybe he'll pull the trigger when it's necessary."

The last was said to Holly with such fury that she flinched. She stared at Archibald, her anger, slow to bloom, coming at last to seize her. He took a step forward, his gun steady at her chest, and plucked her revolver from its holster and handed it over to Borders.

"I leave her to you," Archibald said. "You leave everything else to me. I promise there won't be any more foul-ups."

Borders took the pistol and pointed it at Holly. "See that there aren't," he said in a tone of clear dismissal. Archibald turned and started to make his way back up the hill. Borders did not look at him, his eyes upon Holly. He smiled at her and, with a wave of his pistol, gestured for her to go inside.

29—IF IT'S BLOOD THEY WANT

"You're not well enough to be about. Those burns still need to be seen to, Clive. I can't let you go."

Doc Evans' face was pinched with concern, his small oval spectacles perched precariously on the end of his nose. He had spent the last hour trying and failing to convince Hestin that he needed more time to heal, that bed rest was the only cure. But Hestin would not hear reason on the matter. Someone had tried to murder him, and he needed to find out who and why. And he needed to do it fast.

"I've got no choice, doc," Hestin said. "Someone tried to kill me last night. They'll know they didn't succeed by now, and I have to figure they'll try again, so I've got to get myself ready."

Evans frowned but did not attempt to dissuade Hestin any further. "I don't know what's happening to this town," he said, shaking his head.

"I've an idea," Hestin said, checking his bandages and pulling on his boots. "They want to make themselves the only law here. Somebody needs to stand up to them and make sure they know the mounted police is the law here. They have to answer for it."

Evans sighed. "This can only end in blood, Clive. That kind of talk, it only ends one way."

"Maybe so," Hestin said, already on his way out the door. "If it's blood they want, they'll get it."

Hestin first returned to the ruins of the detachment to see what remained to be salvaged. There was little left beyond a still-smoking husk of ash-colored timbers. All his possessions were gone, though he had little to his name here, beyond a few letters, books, and keepsakes. His serge jacket and pillbox hat were gone, as well as his dress uniform, but new ones could be ordered soon enough. More importantly, given his perilous current circumstances, his pistol and rifle were somewhere in those remains. They would have to be replaced.

After checking the stable next to the detachment, which, miraculously, had been untouched by the fire, and assuring himself that he and Cavanaugh's horses were still present and accounted for, he went to the general store. There he procured himself a new pistol and rifle, along with ammunition, a jacket, pants and shirt, and a hat. The sooner he got out of these singed clothes, the better his frame of mind would be. All of these purchases he bought on credit, telling Walter, the proprietor, that the mounted police would cover any expenses once word had reached them.

From there, he went to the Rose Hotel, found Ann Galvert in the public room, and asked for a room.

"We'd be glad to give you a room, constable. To both you and the lieutenant."

"Much obliged," Hestin said, wondering again what had become of Cavanaugh. The lieutenant had made himself absent before the fire and had not appeared to see how his constable fared after escaping the blaze. It was enough to make a man suspicious. "He'll see to himself. And, of course, you can charge the mounted police for the expenses."

"I wouldn't think of it, constable," Ann said firmly.

"We help out those who've been put out in this community. We're glad to help out folks like you who do so much for this town."

Hestin nodded. "All the same, be sure to charge the mounted police."

He went up to his room, changed into his new clothes, and loaded both the pistol and the rifle. The rifle he hid near his bed and the pistol he put into the holster on his belt. Setting his new hat upon his head, he went out into the street and made his way to the Last Chance Saloon.

There were only a handful of patrons at the Last Chance, unsurprising given that it was not yet noon. Harold Morton was manning the bar, and he watched Hestin enter with a watchful eye, nervously busying himself with cleaning the counter as though he had been caught doing something wrong. He was not the only one watching Hestin as he made his way across the saloon. Everyone looked up from the drinking and gambling and flirting to look him over. As he passed by tables, he could hear them fall to whispering, and he had to resist a smile.

Hestin went to the bar, where Harold would not meet his eye. "Can I get you a drink, constable?"

"I'm on duty," Hestin said, making a show of looking across the whole room.

"Sure, sure," Harold said. "What can I do for you, then?"

Hestin ignored him for the moment, looking at the individual faces of the patrons to see what they might tell him, if anything. Finally, he turned back to Harold, judging he had made him wait long enough.

"You haven't seen Lieutenant Cavanaugh about, have you?"

Harold swallowed loudly and blinked, looking down at the bar. He shook his head, exhaling loudly. "Nope. Nope. Haven't at all. He wasn't caught up in that fire too, was he?"

Hestin shook his head. "No, he wasn't there when it started. And I haven't seen him since. But I thought I might find him here."

"Why would you think that, constable?" Harold said, a little too quickly. "Your kind don't come around here much, you know."

"I know."

Hestin stared directly at Harold, forcing him to meet his gaze. Harold's eyes darted back and forth from Hestin's face to upstairs where the girls' rooms were.

"Well, he ain't been here, constable. And I haven't seen him."

Hestin nodded. "Well, you'll let me know if you do, though?"

Harold bobbed his head. "Sure thing."

Hestin turned to the side, one eye on Harold, one on the dozen or so patrons, all surreptitiously watching his exchange with Harold with great interest. "Harold, you know Horace Goodstone?" he said, as if the question had just occurred to him.

Harold jumped at the question, looking about frantically for some means of escape. Finding none, he said, "He's a farmer out near Rosedale, right?"

"That's right," Hestin said. "Someone took a shot at him the other day."

"That right? Huh," Harold said, shaking his head.

"You know of any reason why someone would be taking a shot at him?"

Harold shook his head again, mystified, his eyes wide and his mouth open.

Hestin nodded, as if Harold had answered his question. He was about to go when he decided to take a shot in the dark. "I'm thinking it has something to do with that fellow Yates that was found hanged in our cells."

He was rewarded with the sight of Harold going very pale. He gulped for air and said, "Why'd you think that?"

Hestin did not answer, smiling at Harold. He turned

from the bar and allowed himself one last look over the saloon before walking out to the street and heading to the stable. His next stop, he decided, would be the Atlas Coal Mine.

30—AN ENCOUNTER

Gene Archibald returned from the Atlas Coal Mine to Wayne along the main road, feeling much better about his prospects than he had that morning. The Amos girl, though alluring in her way, had proven the cause of too many vexing troubles. She could not be trusted, and worse, she could not be controlled. Above all else, Archibald needed to be in command of whatever situation he found himself in, and with her he was not. She was willful.

Borders would deal with her in his own particular way, the details of which Archibald felt better not knowing. The important thing was that she would not be causing him trouble any longer and he could start to put things to right.

The most pressing issue facing him was that damnable constable, who was proving to be as difficult to control as the Amos girl. Somehow the man had survived the detachment fire, which only proved to Archibald that some things he had to handle himself, as much as he disliked involving himself directly in such matters. As with Yates and the problems he posed, the constable, it seemed, would require someone with an attention to detail.

As he was pondering how he would manage the problem of the constable, he saw a rider approaching in the distance. The man was not immediately recognizable. He wore a dark felt hat with a narrow brim and a tan jacket. Something about the way he rode, upright and straight, made Archibald uneasy, but he dismissed it as foolishness and pressed on. He needed to be getting back to the saloon. Harold, left to his own devices, would drink half the stock and burn the place down without noticing.

When the rider was near enough that they could see each other, Archibald brought his horse to a halt in surprise. It was the constable, though he was not wearing his uniform. *Of course he isn't, you damned fool,* Archibald thought. *It went up in smoke with the rest of the detachment.* To cover his discomposure, Archibald loosened his reins and approached the constable. As he came abreast of the other man, he pulled up his mount and nodded deeply, almost bowing.

"Constable," he said. "I'm surprised to see you about after last night. I hear it was a near thing."

The constable, not bothering to disguise his animosity, pulled his horse short. "Near enough," he said.

Archibald wet his lips. His earlier good feeling vanished with the appearance of Hestin, as did the sense that he was in control of events. This moment now felt dangerous, as though it might proceed in any direction, if he wasn't careful. He resisted the urge to let his hand stray from his reins to the gun at his hip.

"Where are you off to?" Archibald said. "I'd have thought you'd be seeing to the detachment. There must be quite a bit of work to setting that all to right."

"There will be," Hestin said. "But it will wait. I'm on my way to the same place you just were."

Archibald swallowed, deciding he would not let the constable bait him. "I see. Well, if you need any help with rebuilding the detachment, you let me know. The Last

Chance stands ready to help."

"Much obliged," Hestin said, and clicked his tongue, urging his horse forward, past Archibald and toward the Atlas Coal Mine.

Archibald remained where he was, watching the constable go. The man would have to be dealt with without delay, he decided. He was far too dangerous to Archibald's prospects to be left alive. With that final thought, he urged his horse toward Wayne.

31—QUESTIONS ASKED AND ANSWERS GIVEN

Someone had to be sent into the mines below to locate the overseer while Clive Hestin waited in his office, trying to contain the restless energy that had seized him since his confrontation with Archibald. No blows had been exchanged, and only a few inconsequential words had passed between them, but everything about the encounter had been charged. Both men had been taking the measure of the other, understanding full well that they were circling nearer and nearer toward a confrontation that would not end with a few words and a tip of the hat.

After what seemed an interminable amount of time, the overseer ducked his head into the office, his face darkened with coal dust. "What can I do for you, constable?"

Hestin did not waste any time in arriving at his point. "Tell me what you know about Gerald Yates."

The overseer frowned, clearly taken aback by the question. "The fellow that hanged himself? All I know is that he was on the road robbing some of the miners. Just like I told you before."

Hestin did not bother to reply. He simply crossed his

arms and stared at overseer, waiting for the truth.

The overseer swallowed. "I swear that's all, constable. I don't know anything else about it."

Still Hestin did not respond, his expression grim and lips pressed tight together.

The overseer tried to match Hestin's gaze, and did so for a time, but eventually he relented. "All right, the fellow was working for Mr. McCauley. I don't know what he was doing for him. But I saw him with Mr. Borders a time or two."

"The robbery story was a frame-up, then?" Hestin said, leaning forward.

"That's right," the overseer said. "Borders brought Yates to us. Told me to send for you and to find some boys who were smart enough to keep their mouths shut and say what they were supposed to."

"Why'd Yates go along with it? He never said he hadn't been stealing from those men."

"I don't know. He didn't say a thing to me or to any of us, so far as I know. Not before. Not after Borders brought him down, either."

Hestin nodded. "I'll need to see those four boys again."

The overseer fled from his office, relief plain on his face, and went to locate the four miners who had sworn Yates was a brigand. Two of them refused to say anything on the matter, in spite of the fact that the overseer had already broken, but the other two echoed what Hestin had already been told. Borders had told them what to say to the law, and offered them a bonus if they went along with the scheme. Yates had not spoken to them that day or before, though both recalled seeing him with Borders on occasion.

"What do you think he was doing with Borders?" Hestin asked.

"He was a hired gun, I'd wager," said one of them, an older fellow, his hair going silver and his eyes hollow.

"Why would Borders need a hired gun around here?"

"Not everything can be solved by law in these parts," the man said with a shrug, as though the answer could not be more obvious.

Hestin supposed that was true, but it still explained nothing. Yates had worked for McCauley, then, but what he was needed for was unclear. Somehow there was a connection between the owner of the Atlas Coal Mine and Gene Archibald as well, for there seemed little doubt who had murdered Yates. Just as there was no question who had sent Holly Amos to shoot at Horace Goodstone, or who had arranged to have the detachment burned down with him in it.

The question remained, as always, why?

Hestin was also certain Archibald had been on his way back from a visit to the house above the mine, no doubt to inform Borders and McCauley of his failures to kill both Goodstone and himself. That was where Hestin had to go now if he was to get the answers he needed.

32—A NEW HIRE

The Last Chance Saloon grew quiet as Gene Archibald pushed through the door, the tables—where no more than a dozen gamblers sat—going still as they saw who it was. That was half the number that was normally here at this hour, and they usually gave him no more than a glance. Archibald pursed his lips and looked around for the source of their unease. Stephen behind the bar looked at him, jerked his head upstairs, and shook his head. He looked pale and nervous. Archibald walked over to him.

"What the hell's going on here?" he said in a low voice.

"Best head upstairs, boss."

Archibald nodded, casting his eyes back over the assembled. No one would meet his eyes. Trouble, then, and the nagging sense of something wrong that had been plaguing him since his brief encounter with the constable only grew. Events were moving quickly, too quickly for him to control, and it threatened to put him at the center of a maelstrom.

His suspicions were proved correct, as he discovered to his dismay, when he went upstairs. There he found Harold Morton standing over Lieutenant Cavanaugh's body, which lay sprawled in the bed. His throat had been cut and he'd been stabbed in the gut, and there was blood spattered across the bed, on the walls, and on the floor. On Harold's clothes as well, Archibald saw as he glanced at him. Harold would not look at him, his eyes intent on the dead policeman, his breathing coming in heavy rasps.

"What the hell happened here?" Archibald said. He had to ask Harold again before he received a reply.

"I had to. I had to. He was gonna tell."

Archibald sighed and shook his head. This was bad. This was very bad. Cavanaugh was his insurance against the mounted police ever getting too interested in what happened in Wayne. With him murdered, they would start listening to Hestin, unless something was done about that. Even if something was—and Archibald intended to make sure there was—the law would investigate the death of their own. The place would be crawling with mounted police.

"Who was he going to tell?" Archibald said, turning his attention back to Harold, careful to keep his voice even.

"The constable. He came around asking questions." It seemed to dawn on Harold whom he was talking to. He turned to look at Archibald. "I didn't tell him nothing, Gene. I swear it. But he knew. He knew everything. He was asking about Yates and Goodstone."

"He was, was he?" Archibald said.

"Yeah. Cavanaugh heard it all. He said it was all over. Couldn't hide anything more from the constable. He said he was through helping you. No gain in it. He was going to save himself. Told me to do the same. But I said I wouldn't do that."

"And you killed him."

"Yeah," Harold said, shaking his head mournfully. "Yeah, I had to."

Archibald put a hand to his temple. He wanted very much to do some grievous harm to this fool and drunkard who, for some reason, was in his employ, but there were the people downstairs to think about.

"Anybody see you?"

Harold thought a moment. "They saw me come up here. And they probably heard everything. But nobody knows he was here. I swear it, Gene."

Archibald shook his head in disgust. "Wait here. Don't leave this room under any circumstances. I'll handle things downstairs."

He turned and went downstairs, leaving Harold to his mournful vigil over the lieutenant's body. As Archibald descended the steps, mindful of the attentive sidelong glances from the assembled below, he considered his options. There were no good ones left to him, that much was clear. The day had spun from his control, and all he could do now was try to minimize the consequences for himself.

Borders would be furious when he heard, but he would be busy with the Amos girl for the day, so it would be some time before he did. Archibald realized he would need to be the one to deliver the bad news, to be able to direct Borders' wrath in useful directions. McCauley's assistant was predictable, if nothing else. Archibald had used that to his advantage before, and he could do so again now, provided he came up with a way to salvage this whole mess. But how to do that?

As he pondered that question, Archibald noticed that Jeremiah James, the mammoth ruffian who had informed him of Holly Amos' involvement in the payroll heist, was leaning against the bar, in conference with Stephen. That heist had set off this particular chain of events, sending all Archibald's carefully guided plans off the rails, leaving him in the straits he was in now. Perhaps Jeremiah could prove useful again.

He walked over to the bar and spoke in an undertone. "Stephen, anyone here see what happened up there?"

Stephen shook his head. "No. Harold went up there and he won't let anyone in the room. The girls tell me he's covered in blood."

"It's a hell of mess, all right. You know who was in there, Stephen?"

The barkeep shook his head. Archibald did not believe him, but let that go for the moment. Stephen knew enough to keep his mouth shut. "Get these folks out of here," Archibald said, jerking his thumb at the tables behind him. "We're closed. The girls have the day off too. They either stay in their rooms or get the hell out. Same goes for you."

Stephen nodded and went around the bar to tell the men at the tables. No questions asked. A good man, Stephen.

Archibald turned to Jeremiah. "You still interested in that job we talked about yesterday?"

Jeremiah smiled. "I'm here, aren't I? I take it there's been an opening."

"There has," Archibald said. "And your first job is upstairs, once these folks are out of here."

33—AT THE MCCAULEY HOUSE

Borders opened the door and registered the presence of Hestin with an impatient sigh. "Constable, what can I do for you?" he said, pushing a hand through his fine hair.

"I was wondering if you could answer some questions for me."

"Are these urgent questions, constable? I don't really have time to spare today. I have some matters to attend to, and tomorrow I have to return to Calgary to report to Mr. McCauley."

Hestin allowed himself a thin smile. "I'm afraid these can't wait. They concern Gerald Yates."

Borders frowned, but stepped back and waved for Hestin to enter the house, closing the door behind him. "Gerald Yates? Oh, the fellow who hanged himself. Surely you've got more important things to attend to at the moment, constable? Wasn't your detachment burned to the ground last night?"

"Yes, and I was in it."

"Not for long, I take it," Borders said, with a smile that left Hestin cold.

He beckoned for Hestin to follow him from the entry into the next room, which was a finely appointed parlor.

Hestin found it difficult not to look at the furniture, or the paintings on the wall, but he kept his gaze upon Borders, who went to a small wooden cabinet and extracted a bottle and two glasses. He filled them both with a measure of liquor and turned back to Hestin, offering one to him.

"I'd think you'd be interested in finding out what happened there, instead of digging up an old matter like the Yates death. I'd understood it was settled."

"Not to my satisfaction," Hestin said, declining the offered drink. "It's my feeling that the two matters are related."

"Really? The fire and the suicide? I fail to see how that could be."

Borders studied the two glasses in his hand. He held up one again, and Hestin again shook his head.

"The fire was deliberately set, with the intention of killing me. I believe Yates was killed as well. He had no rope on him to hang himself. And I believe the same man was behind both these acts."

Borders relented, setting the glass atop a table beside the cabinet. He studied Hestin through narrowed eyes, swirling the liquor in his glass, nodding to himself. "You do, do you? And who might this man be?"

"Gene Archibald."

Borders took a sip of whiskey. "The proprietor of the saloon in Wayne?"

"You know very well who he is," Hestin said.

"I can assure you, I do not frequent saloons, constable."

"That may well be, but I met him on my way here. And he was not visiting the mine."

"He was not visiting here, either, constable. I can assure you, I don't mix with those sorts."

Borders seemed distracted for a moment, as though he could hear something in the distance. Hestin listened as well, and thought he could hear something. A scream or a yell, a woman's voice, though well muffled. It came again, and this time he was certain it was there. He resisted a shudder.

Borders was looking at him carefully, but Hestin could not tell if he suspected the constable of hearing the woman's cries. Hestin frowned, as though considering the other man's words. "Is that so?"

Borders drained his glass and took Hestin by the arm, leading from the parlor back toward the door. "I can assure you that it is so," he said. "Now, if that is all the questions you have, I really must ask you to leave. I have much to attend to."

Hestin allowed himself to be led to the door, but once there, he shook himself free. He could no longer hear the cries of the woman, though he listened intently. Borders returned his gaze calmly, his face showing none of his thoughts. Hestin cast about for some question or pretext that would allow him to stay longer. He had nothing but a theory, which Borders had denied, and a little evidence. Nothing that would stand up in a court of law, not with the lawyers Borders could no doubt hire.

He had come here hoping to shake some answers loose, but Borders was not like the overseer or the miners. He was not intimidated by a constable of the Northwest Mounted Police. That left them at an impasse, which under normal circumstances would have been fine. Hestin had seen enough of the man that his suspicions were confirmed. It was a just a matter of finding the proof he needed. But he had no time for that now. He he had to discover where the woman was hidden and help her if he could.

"I just need a moment more of your time," Hestin said.

"I'm afraid not," Borders said. "It's really quite impossible. I'm happy to answer any questions you may have upon my return from Calgary. But unless you have some evidence, or something that would show how any of these unfortunate events relate in any way to myself or Mr. McCauley, our conversation is at an end."

He took a further step, herding Hestin closer to the door. The constable stood firm, refusing to be cowed. "I have all the proof I need," he said. "Now I have some more questions and I expect some answers."

34—IN THE CELLAR

Darkness surrounded Holly, with only the odd hint of light finding its way to where she sat. Her wrists burned from the ropes that bound her, and her back hurt from sitting in one position on this chair that seemed purpose-built to make her uncomfortable. The smell of earth and the creak of footsteps on the floor above her were the only things that identified where she was being held, in the cellar beneath the vast house, the possession and plaything of a madman.

"Rest here awhile," Borders had told her after he bound her. "I'll deal with you when I am at my *leisure*."

The way he said the last word curdled her blood, and she had instinctively fought against the ropes. To no avail. Her only accomplishment on that front had been rubbing her wrists raw. The knots were tight and the rope had no give to it. Her arms ached from her efforts and from the way they were bent over the back of the chair.

She had no sense of how much time had passed since Borders had put her here. In the darkness, there was nothing she could use to judge its passage beyond the creak of the bastard's footsteps above her. He seemed to be alone in the house, to judge by his solitary footfalls—

not that it mattered, given her current predicament. She alternated between frantic attempts to free herself, certain that her time was up and he would descend upon her soon, and resigned and wrathful despair, where she awaited her doom and cursed that scum Archibald for betraying her.

How had she not seen it coming? Of course he would believe Jeremiah James' tale, true as it might be. If she had killed Goodstone as he had asked, would he have spared her?

Her knife was still tucked into the back pocket of her pants, so tantalizingly near her hands that she wanted to weep. Borders had missed it, not bothering to search her, and that had been a mistake. But not one that she was able to make him pay for. If there were any give to the rope at all, she would be free.

Above her, she heard the footfalls across the floor again. They disappeared and reappeared a moment later, followed by another set of footsteps. The sound of muffled voices reached her, though she couldn't distinguish who was speaking. Despite that, she decided she had nothing to lose, and began to scream and cry for help. If the newcomer heard her and was not in league with Borders, he might do something to save her.

As she yelled and screamed, the voices drifted away from the room above. Holly yelled in frustration. She fought the ropes feverishly, struggling for whatever tiny bit of give she could find. But there was still none, and she fell silent, giving up again.

The voices came again, seemingly far away from where her chair was, possibly a room or two over. She resumed screaming, hoping against hope that she would be heard. The voices went silent above her, and she felt a surge of triumph that vanished a moment later as they resumed, though even fainter now. She closed her eyes and tried to still her ragged breathing.

There was no one to help her but herself, she realized,

and so long as Borders' visitor remained above, she had time. She needed to be sure she used it well.

As fighting against the knots had proved ineffective, she decided to try to topple the chair to see if that would change things. She rocked the chair from side to side, tipping it a little further each time, fighting the urge to try to right herself. It took several attempts before she managed to push herself past the point of no return, and the chair fell, leaving her on her side.

Her left arm was pinned and numb with pain from the fall, but there did seem to be more give to the rope. She began to wriggle against the chair, trying to shimmy herself up its back so that her arms would be able to move better. It was exhausting work, but slowly she managed to work herself free. Having done so, she rolled herself onto her side and contorted her arms enough to dig her hands into her back pocket and pull out the knife.

It took her several tries to get the pocketknife open, as she repeatedly dropped the knife to the floor and had to pick it up again. Even once she had the blade open, she had to turn it so she cut the ropes. She cut herself twice in the process, swearing under her breath in frustration, but at last managed to get the knife turned and set in her hands so she could cut her bonds.

As she did so, the murmurs above her, which had been intermittent but always present, went quiet. She froze, wondering if the guest had left and if Borders would now turn to her. Footsteps creaked across the floor, coming toward her, and she shuddered and began to saw away at the rope as fast as she could manage.

35—BORDERS

For an instant, and only an instant, the calm exterior Borders exhibited vanished and Hestin caught a glimpse of the man behind it. He saw fury and violence, both tightly contained. Then they were gone and Borders was gazing impassively at him, making no move to force him from the house.

Hestin swallowed. He had bought some time and now had to make it count. "Do you know Horace Goodstone?"

Borders shook his head, not bothering to hide his displeasure.

"He's a landholder near Rosedale," Hestin said. "An honest fellow. If there was a spur line from the railroad to the mine, it would go along his land. Somebody took a shot at him the other day. Almost killed him."

Borders gestured with his hand. "Why does any of this matter to me in the least?"

"The railroad is important to Mr. McCauley, I would imagine."

"To be sure. It is essential to the continued feasibility of this mine. Mr. McCauley has made a large investment here, on the assumption that the railroad will go through. That it's been delayed as long as it has has been a great hardship."

Hestin only half listened to Borders' reply as he tried and failed to hear something else from the woman. She must be in the cellar below. He wondered if there was an entrance somewhere outside the house. Most homes would have that, but this mansion was not most homes.

"Well, when I talked to Mr. Goodstone about the matter, he told me he was convinced his shooting was related to the railroad and the mine. He said a representative of the railroad had been to see him about selling his land and had threatened him when he refused to sell."

Borders shook his head. "I can tell you that was not me." He stepped past Hestin and pulled the door open. They were standing very close to each other, eye to eye and near enough to touch.

Hestin did not move. "I wasn't saying it was. I asked him to describe the man. It sounded to me like Gerald Yates."

"Well then, he was being threatened by a known thief and a scoundrel. Mr. Yates was no representative of Mr. McCauley. If he was claiming so, he was lying."

Hestin leaned forward, his manner genial but insistent. "Your overseer and some of the miners below have all told me they saw Yates with you on more than one occasion. They've also told me that you paid them to sing me their tale about him being a thief."

"Surely you don't believe men of that ilk over someone of my standing," Borders said, with a dismissive wave of his empty hand.

The other was holding the empty glass, but Hestin was not watching it. By the time he realized what was happening Borders was bringing it down upon his forehead. The glass was heavy and the blow stunned Hestin, sending him reeling. Another blow from the glass, this time to his nose, sent him to the floor. His vision was clouded with light, and his head, already tender from the boot heel he had received the night before, was in agony. He clutched it and doubled over on the floor, worried that he would vomit. Blood dribbled from his nose, and its aching suggested that it might be broken.

Somewhere above him, Borders sighed. Hestin felt the gun being taken from his holster and went still.

"This would have been much easier for you if you'd taken the drink I'd offered. I'd prefer that Archibald deal with you, but apparently that is beyond his capabilities. No matter, though. It's not beyond mine."

Hestin heard Borders leaving the room, disappearing somewhere within the house. Knowing this might be his only chance, Hestin tried to get to his feet, but fell to the floor, overwhelmed by nausea and dizziness. His vision was clouded and swirling, and he moaned to himself. On his knees, he crawled forward to what he thought was the still-open door and the porch where his horse was tied. He did not have long before Borders returned with whatever he intended to use to end Hestin's life.

"Going somewhere?" Borders said.

Hestin looked up, blinking. His vision resolved itself a little and he saw Borders peering down at him, a large knife in his hand.

"I think you're heading the wrong direction," Borders said as Hestin realized, with a sinking terror, he was in the parlor.

Borders leaned down and grasped Hestin by the hair, dragging him into a sitting position. Hestin groaned in agony, swinging wildly with his hands, trying to ward the other man off. His hands struck at Borders' legs, but had no effect upon him.

"Do you know that the Indians use these knives to scalp a man?" Borders said, studying the edge of the blade as it glinted in the sunlight. "I think that would be a fitting end for a man like you. You're supposed to be pacifying the savages, not causing men like me trouble. I am the future of this territory."

Hestin looked up at Borders, shuddering at the sight of his malevolent smile. His head was in agony, but he knew he had to fight now, or it would get much, much worse. He tried to push himself to his feet, throwing his weight in Borders' direction, hoping to knock him off balance. Borders simply moved with him, stepping out of the way and letting him lunge into the air and fall to the floor. Before Hestin could even think of scrambling away, Borders had hold of his hair and was pulling him up again, the knife ready to cut.

Hestin looked up wide-eyed at Borders, paralyzed by fear. Borders stared at him, seeming to feast on that terror, his smile growing broader. It vanished a moment later, a confused look coming over his face. He took an unsteady step forward and exhaled softly, dropping Hestin and his knife to the floor.

"Come on," Holly Amos said, appearing from behind Borders, a bloody knife in her hand.

She grabbed him by the shoulder and dragged him forward, urging him to his feet. He managed to rise, though he needed to lean on her, and glanced back to see that Borders had fallen to the floor and was muttering something to himself.

"Never mind him," Holly said in his ear. "We've got to get moving."

He nodded and followed her out the door into the bright sunlight.

36—A BLOODY DISCOVERY

For the second time that day, Archibald rode his horse down the road to the Atlas Coal Mine, Jeremiah James at his side. He felt now that he had matters under control again. Jeremiah had dealt with Harold, and they had left the bodies in the room for one of the girls to discover. Once the troublesome constable had been dealt with, there would be no one who would dare contradict whatever claims he made to the mounted police when they arrived.

That would be several days at least, depending on how soon word was sent to them. More than enough time to deal with the constable and set things right with Borders and his master McCauley. Archibald did not want to delay, though. The time to strike was now, while the constable was outside town and hopefully not expecting an attack.

When they came near the mine, they took a trail that branched off into the twisting crevasses of the badlands and hobbled the horses out of sight. They continued on foot, staying in the hills above the road to the mine, where they would be able to see if the constable passed back this way. He did not, and eventually the trail met the path that led from the mine up to the McCauley estate. That, Archibald was certain, was where the constable was, trying to squeeze whatever information he could from Borders. He would find that well quite dry.

As they came in sight of the house, they could see a horse tied up to the porch. The door to the house stood open, which was odd. Archibald motioned for Jeremiah to be ready with the rifle he carried and they came forward. The horse, which Archibald felt certain was the constable's, stirred as they walked past. Otherwise, the only sound was their own steps upon the porch.

The quiet was unsettling, and Archibald motioned for Jeremiah to keep watch from the doorway while he investigated within. In the parlor, he found Borders sprawled on the floor in a pool of his own blood. He returned quickly to where Jeremiah was standing, rifle at the ready, eyes upon the horizon.

"Borders is dead," he said. "No sign of the constable."

"You think he's hiding somewhere out here?" Jeremiah said.

Archibald scanned the hillside. It was open, with nowhere for the constable to hide and nowhere for him to pass by without them spotting him. Behind the house, where he and Holly had descended earlier in the day, it was even more exposed. If he was climbing up into the hills, they would be able to see him.

"Could be," he said. "Could be he saw us coming and wants us to think that."

Jeremiah nodded. "What do you want to do?"

Archibald stepped out of the door, closing it behind him. "Let's have a look around back and make sure he's not hightailing it out of here. If we don't see him, then we know where he is."

Jeremiah nodded and smiled, and they started to circle the house, each going around one side.

37—CAT AND MOUSE

Holly had not stopped to think when she first spotted Gene Archibald and Jeremiah James making their way up the hill toward the McCauley house—she had acted. Taking the still-stunned Hestin by the arm, she fled around the veranda to the back of the house. She crouched with him under a window, gathering her breath and her thoughts, trying to figure out how they might escape this situation.

She could hear the two men go up the steps and into the house. They would find Borders and then they would come looking for them. She cursed at herself for not retreating into the house, where Borders would have weapons, including her own and the constable's. Now they were out here, with nowhere to run, and only a knife to defend themselves against two men with guns who would not hesitate to use them.

As she lifted her head near the window, the better to hear what was happening within, Holly rubbed her wrists, which were raw from her efforts to escape. Hestin met her eyes with a focused gaze, putting her mind somewhat at ease. She could not face these two and mind him at the same time. The constable raised an eyebrow in question, and she shrugged in response.

She could hear Archibald's voice, though she could not make out what he was saying, followed by Jeremiah's. The door closed and footsteps started toward them on either side of the veranda. Holly looked blankly out at the hills behind the house as though they might have an answer. They did not, for if they ran there, Jeremiah would be able to pick them off with ease, though he was only half the shot she was.

Hestin was moving before she realized it, going to the door and quietly turning the handle and pulling it open. He motioned for her to enter, which she did, and he followed her, closing it soundlessly. They crept through the house, staying low and out of sight of the windows, going as quickly as they dared. At the door, they could hear Archibald and Jeremiah meet and discuss what to do next.

Holly paused as they passed through the parlor and by Borders' still body. She searched him for a pistol, digging in his coat pockets and around his belt, but came away with nothing but blood on her hands. The constable was by the front door, and he waved insistently at her to follow him, which she did reluctantly. They slipped out the front door as silently as they had come in the back and started down the steps.

38—PICKING UP THE TRAIL

Archibald pointed at the cellar door as they entered the house. He figured the constable must have fled there when he saw them coming, and now was trapped. They dug up a lantern from the kitchen, lit it, and went below, Archibald carrying it and Jeremiah following with his gun ready. But they did not find the constable in the cellar, only a chair and some ropes that had been cut up.

"She's with him," Archibald said, kicking at the ropes with his foot.

"I thought you said this Borders was going to finish her."

"He was. Obviously, he didn't get the chance." Archibald sighed. "We'll split up when we get upstairs."

Jeremiah nodded and they went above. Before they had a chance to split up, Archibald glanced in the parlor to where Borders lay on the floor. Something about the body made him go into the room to look closer. It was not in the same position it had been when he last looked at it, he was certain. He held up a hand to alert Jeremiah to be ready, and crouched over the body.

Borders' clothes were twisted oddly about his frame, but that was not what got Archibald's attention. There were bloody footprints leading from the body to the front door.

"Dammit," he said, leaping to his feet. "They've gone out the front door."

He raced to the door, Jeremiah following, and headed out to the veranda. Descending down the winding path to the mine was the horse with two figures seated upon it. Archibald looked at Jeremiah, who did not need to be told. He had already raised his rifle to his shoulder and was taking aim.

39—INTO THE HILLS

The first shot missed by so much that Holly wondered if Jeremiah was shooting in the wrong direction. The second was very near, so close that she could almost feel its passage as it sang through the air. The third struck the horse in one its legs, panicking it and spilling her to the ground. As she rolled over to look up, she saw the constable kick himself free of the limping animal, just as the fourth bullet echoed across the badlands.

He fell to the ground and lay there for a moment, making Holly wonder if Jeremiah had gotten lucky again. But Hestin finally looked up at her, shaking himself a little as if to check that all his bones were intact. Holly had already done so, and she nodded to indicate that she was all right.

"We've got to find some cover," she called out. "If we give him enough chances to get his range, he'll hit one of us eventually."

Hestin nodded and scrambled to his feet, fleeing down the slope. Holly waited a second, turning back to look at the house, before following suit. Hestin turned off the main road down a trail that she barely noticed that led to a crevasse between two hills, which would provide them with some cover. She followed, the way becoming so steep that they both slid down on their backsides rather than try to stay on their feet.

There were no more shots, but she knew Archibald and Jeremiah would not be far behind. The last thing she had seen before fleeing was Archibald running across the hilltop as Jeremiah tried to sight them in from the porch. That thought spurred her on as she followed the constable deeper into the hills and coulees of the badlands.

40—THE BADLANDS

Hestin's arm ached where he'd landed on it after being tossed from the horse. He stretched his arm out and brought it back, trying to halt any stiffness from setting in. The Amos woman watched him, a distant expression on her face, both of them gathering their breath after their headlong flight. Her wrists were red with what looked like rope burns and one eye was dark with blood, Hestin assumed from her fall from the horse, but otherwise she appeared fine.

Somewhere above them were the two men pursuing them. He'd gone off the trail as soon as possible, hoping to make their pursuit more difficult. There was little in the way of cover here. No trees and hardly any brush. Just a series of hills descending like giant, misshapen stairs toward the river valley. So long as they stayed off the plateaus and kept descending, he hoped they would be difficult to spot.

"What should we do?" Holly said, wiping sweat from her forehead and looking up above.

They were at the bottom of a hill, with another plateau before them, which they would have to cross to reach their next descent. Neither of them strayed from the steep hillside, which was scarred with dry streambeds where winter runoff had carved away at the dirt, and which they had used to slide down the hillside.

Hestin followed her gaze, but the slope above was empty. "We have to keep going," he said, "and try to get to the river valley. There's more cover there. Maybe we can lose them, or at least get to somebody who can help."

"There's another way," Holly said, still looking up the hillside. "We split up and try to hide somewhere here. Get the jump on them."

Hestin shook his head. "We've only got your knife. And both of them have guns. It would be risking a lot."

Holly sighed. "Nothing ventured, constable. I could hide and you could keep going down. Maybe I get the jump on them, maybe I don't. Either way, it slows them down and lets you get down to the valley."

"I won't leave you to that fate."

Holly gave a bitter laugh. "What nobility. I can handle myself. Isn't bringing them to justice more important?"

Hestin hesitated, feeling his face flush. He always found himself uncomfortable around Holly, as though he was missing some joke that she was telling at his expense. "For now, I'm just worried about us getting out of this mess alive. Justice can wait."

"Even mine?"

Was she taunting him for his inability to arrest her after she had shot at Horace Goodstone? If he had, Borders would surely have scalped him, or he would have burned up in the fire. That did not excuse Hestin's failure, not in his mind. Especially since he was fairly certain she had not killed Morris Danforth in self-defense, as she had claimed. And there was still the matter of her possible involvement in the payroll heist and the murder of those two men.

All that could wait. Just as he could wait to thank her for saving him twice. None of it would matter if they couldn't escape this predicament.

"Let's just get ourselves out of this mess. The rest we

can deal with later."

Holly nodded. "Fine. But we play this my way."

Hestin opened his mouth to argue, but before he could say anything, she cut him off. "I'm the one with the knife here. And you're moving that arm like its hurt pretty bad, to say nothing of your nose. And I know these fellows a lot better than you."

Hestin could not argue with that. Reluctantly, he nodded. "What's your play, then?"

Holly's eyes lingered on the slope above them. She stood, pushing herself back from the hillside. A bullet whined through the air, striking the hill above them, creating an explosion of dust and a cascade of dirt down to their feet. Holly returned to the hillside, pressing her back against it.

"Did you see where?" she said.

Hestin nodded. "He's up on that ridge." He pointed at the hill beside the one they had just come down, which jutted out farther than the one they clung to.

"I see him," Holly said, frowning and looking around. "Looks like it's just him. Archibald must be coming down somewhere else."

Hestin craned his head up to look above, but Archibald was not there—he had not come to the edge of the ridge where they could see him. Hestin winced as another shot stirred the dust above them.

Holly shook her head. "We're just damn lucky he's always too drunk to shoot straight."

Hestin crouched down, not at all reassured. "What happens when the liquor wears off?"

Holly did not even glance back at him. "He gets angry."

He wanted to ask her how she knew this Jeremiah James, but that was another question best left for later.

"We should get out of his range," he said, starting to move away from the hill Jeremiah was perched on, being careful to stay close to the hillside, where it would be hard for him to pick them out.

"We already are," Holly said, but followed him, stopping every now and again to study the hillside.

The shooting continued sporadically as they went along, none of the shots coming anywhere close to hitting them. That did little to salve Hestin's jangled nerves. In the space of a night and a day, he had been beaten and left to burn, beaten and nearly scalped, and now was being shot at by one man, while another lurked somewhere nearby, waiting to pounce upon them. At least, he thought, they couldn't bring their horses down here.

He hurried ahead, hoping to get around the lip of the hill and out of sight of the rise Jeremiah was on.

"Wait," Holly said, and he stopped to look at her. She was still facing the hillside where Jeremiah was. "He's herding us," she said. "He knows he can't hit us, but he wants to try to scare us into going this way."

Hestin wet his lips, pondering the implications of this.

Holly looked at him. "I've got an idea. You're not going to like it."

"What is it?"

"You make a break for it. Run across the plateau and down the next hill. We know that Jeremiah can't hit you. And we force Gene to do something. Does he follow you? Or does he come deal with me? Either way, we'll know where he is."

"Sure, but even if we do know where he is, there's not much we can do about it."

"There's always something," Holly said, though she did not elaborate on what that might be.

Hestin nodded, failing to find any argument that might persuade Holly otherwise. "All right. What if Archibald doesn't show himself?"

"Then I follow you. I figure if Archibald doesn't show, Jeremiah will start coming down the slope. That's the main thing. We can't let him get in range with that rifle."

"Right," Hestin said.

He looked at Holly one last time, in the hopes that she

might come up with some other plan that did not involve him running across open country. She nodded and gave him an encouraging smile. Taking a deep breath, he jumped to his feet and began to run across the plateau to the next ridge.

41—SURE SHOT

Holly looked from the ridge where Jeremiah still lay sighting in his rifle to where the constable was fleeing across the open hilltop. He was moving at an angle that took him further from the rifle's range, but Jeremiah made no move to alter his position. Likely he was still trying to figure out what exactly Holly was up to, since he could still see her remaining where she was, and wondering how he could let Archibald know.

She half expected to see Archibald emerge from somewhere beyond the curve of the hill that she and Hestin had descended, racing in pursuit of the constable. But Archibald was too smart for that. He would know she was here, somewhere, and would be wondering what she was up to as well.

Hestin made it to the hill's edge and disappeared below. She nodded and smiled. That was good. It would force them to do something, if they wanted to stop him from getting to the river valley. Hopefully she would be able to glean some advantage from it when they did.

As if in response to the constable's disappearance, Jeremiah moved from his perch atop the hill and began to slide down to the adjacent plateau. Soon he would be at her level, and in range to shoot her—if he was any kind of shot, which he wasn't. She would have to either follow the constable or go somewhere else to ensure Jeremiah didn't get close enough to where he might actually hit her.

After thinking about it for a moment, she began to climb back up the hill, staying within one of the washouts where rain or winter runoff had coursed down the bare hillside. It was hard work getting back up, and she had to move without ceasing. Every foothold was tenuous, the earth threatening to crumble under her feet, sending her back down to where she had started.

She was perhaps a third of the way up when a shout from below halted her ascent. Archibald had emerged from the far side of the hill and was looking up at her, a pistol in his hand. He moved directly below her, glancing from her precarious perch to the plateau's edge, where the constable had just disappeared, as though he was unsure of whom he should go after. While he was still frozen with indecision, Holly acted, catapulting herself off the hillside and down toward him.

Archibald realized too late what she was doing and was unable to get out of the way in time. Her knee caught him in the head, pitching him forward, so that when she landed, he was beneath her. She tried to carry her momentum into a roll, but got tangled up with Archibald and came to an abrupt and agonizing halt at the bottom of the hill, with him beneath her.

The air went from her lungs and she struggled for breath, blinking furiously and trying to keep her vision from going, knowing Jeremiah would have seen what happened and be coming for her. There was a sharp pain in her left arm that worried her, but she ignored it as best she could and worked to untangle herself from Archibald. He lay still beneath her—dead, for all she knew.

A shot echoed across the valley and she managed to look up. Jeremiah stood some distance from her, though probably still near enough to be able to shoot her, his rifle pointed at the sky.

"Get away from him, girl," he shouted, and fired another shot.

Holly did not move, knowing he wouldn't dare to shoot at her for fear of hitting Archibald. She cast her eyes around, trying to find where Archibald's pistol had gone, and finally spotted where it had been thrown, at least two paces from his body.

"Get away from him, Holly," Jeremiah said, rifle still pointed at the sky. "You're finished, girl."

He started walking toward her. Once he was near enough, it wouldn't matter whether he shot her—he was strong enough to overpower her, and they both knew it. She stayed where she was, watching him approach. An ugly smile came over his face as she waited, and he lowered his rifle, pointing it to the ground.

As soon as he did that, she was on her feet, scrambling across the ground to where Archibald's pistol lay. She had it in hand by the time Jeremiah managed to get his rifle back up to his shoulder. He looked surprised to see a gun in her hand and fired in a panic, his shot going well wide of her. Holly took her time to aim and pulled the trigger before he could fire again. The bullet caught him in the shoulder, sending him to the ground with a grunt of surprise.

Holly ran over to where he lay, kicking the rifle away before he could get ahold of it again. She stepped back from him as he rolled over, squirming in agony, leveling her pistol at his head.

"Just finish it," he said in a strangled voice and she prepared to pull the trigger.

"Don't," the constable called to her as he clambered over the ridge to join her on the plateau. "Let him face the law."

Holly looked from the constable to the contorted face of Jeremiah before lowering the pistol.

42—IN THE STABLES

It was nightfall by the time Holly and Hestin brought Jeremiah James and Gene Archibald back to Wayne. Doc Evans was summoned to see to their injuries, and Hestin deputized a few men he trusted to keep watch on them at the doc's house until morning, when he would send someone to get word to Calgary about the detachment fire and all the other happenings. He and Holly returned to the Rose Hotel, both of them exhausted and desperate for sleep.

But Stephen Blackmore, bartender at the Last Chance, was there waiting for them. "I think you should come to the saloon," he said. "There's something you need to see."

Hestin nodded and followed Stephen, with Holly coming along despite him telling her not to. Hestin did not have the energy to argue with her, and so let it be. When they came to the saloon, it was closed, which Stephen said was on the Archibald's orders. He unlocked the door and led them upstairs to the girls' rooms, where a few worried-looking women stood on the balcony. They parted at the sight of Stephen, who led Hestin and Holly into one of the rooms. There was a lantern lit, illuminating a terrible scene. The bed, the walls, and the floor were all streaked with blood.

"Maude told me she saw Gene and that big fellow taking the lieutenant and Harold downstairs and the out the back," Stephen said, jerking his thumb at one of the women who were crowding around the entrance to the room.

"Where are the bodies?" Hestin said.

Stephen shrugged, but one of the woman said, "Stables out back, I'd guess."

Hestin took a lantern, and he and Holly went to the stables. In one of the stalls, they found Cavanaugh and Harold Morton's bodies piled atop other. Cavanaugh had been stabbed and Harold shot. Hestin shook his head sorrowfully, and Holly would not meet his eyes. He wondered if she had known, if these murders occurred before she had been imprisoned by Borders.

Hestin went inside to get Stephen to help deal with the bodies, sending one of the girls to wake the mortician. When the bodies were safely in his care, Hestin went to bed, unable to stay awake any longer, his thoughts suffused by a deep melancholy at all the destruction of these last days. His final thought as he went to sleep was to wonder what would remain when he awoke.

43—A MISSING BODY

The constable was eating breakfast alone in the public room of the Rose when Holly emerged from her room. He looked as though he wanted to be alone, his expression morose, but Holly sat across from him anyway.

"You got a busy day ahead of you," she said.

He looked up from his plate of food, not replying. Ann Galvert came and brought her a plate of eggs, beans, and toast and a cup of coffee. Only when she had bustled on to another table did Hestin speak.

"Did you know about the fire?"

Holly shook her head, shoveling a mouthful of eggs into her mouth. "I just saw it. I don't know why I figured someone was still in the detachment. Maybe something that Gene said made me think it. The way he said it, you know. But I went to look."

"Why'd you pull me out?" Hestin said.

Holly shrugged. "Why'd you let me walk away by the river?"

Hestin looked away.

After a moment, Holly said, "I'll go down to the mine today and see to Borders if you want."

Hestin looked at her sharply. "Why?"

"You got a busy day ahead of you."

"I do," he said. "But why are you willing to help me?"

"I'm not a terrible person, constable. Not entirely, anyway. You got a lot on your plate with Archibald and Jeremiah. Borders is just one more thing. But I can take care of it."

Hestin pushed aside his plate. "And what do you want in return? Me to look the other way about you working for Archibald? You're going to have to testify, you know. They may decide to charge you for whatever part you had in this."

Holly's nostrils flared. "I'm not asking for any favor. Not from you. Not from anyone. And I've done more than enough already to get a favor from you, without needing to be cleaning up that mess at the coal mine. So do you want my help or not?"

Hestin seemed taken aback by her anger. "It would be a big help if you could go out to see to Borders. Thank you."

Holly nodded, and they finished their breakfast in silence. When she was done, she went to the Last Chance, borrowed one of Archibald's horses, and rode to the house above the Atlas Coal Mine. There she found a bloodstained floor in the parlor, but otherwise no sign that Borders had ever been there.

That was unsettling, for she had been certain he was dead when she had searched his body for a gun. It was possible that he was still alive. She had only been near him a few frantic seconds and had paid no mind to him or his condition. Obviously he had recovered enough to vacate the premises.

Still, he couldn't have gone far, and so she set about conducting a search of the area. First, she climbed up the hill behind the house to where she and Archibald had left their horses the morning before. There was no sign of the horse, or anything else beyond the windswept plains. In the hills below, she eventually came across the horses

Archibald and Jeremiah must have been riding the day before, but there was no trace of Borders to be found.

She kept at it for the better part of a day, wandering among the hills and asking a few of the miners what they had seen that day. Eventually she began to ask herself what she was doing. This was the law's job, not hers. The constable had as much as said he wanted to arrest her, and here she was running around the territory for him to no purpose. As strange and unsettling as it might be that Borders had vanished, it was no concern of hers, and as the sun began its descent and a chill began to creep into the air, she turned her horse toward Wayne.

44—PARTING WAYS

Three days after a rider was dispatched to notify the mounted police in Calgary of what had happened in Wayne, Sergeant Dugald Nettlecamp arrived to take command of the investigation. Riding into town beside him was Mortimer McCauley.

Both men praised Constable Hestin for his work in exposing the criminal activities of Gene Archibald and Heathcliff Borders. McCauley declared himself ignorant of the scheme to buy up all the land along the proposed railway spur lines, claiming that he had ordered Gerald Yates fired when he discovered that he had been threatening locals if they didn't sell to Borders. He did not explain why he had lied to Hestin about knowing Yates when the constable had come to speak to him.

It was clear that Nettlecamp had already decided McCauley was innocent of these schemes, and with Borders gone and Archibald refusing to say anything, Hestin had nothing beyond his own suspicions to say otherwise. For once, he decided it would be best not to speak, and to let matters take their course. Archibald and Jeremiah James would hang, and with Borders gone, there would be no one left to carry out the land grab. If

McCauley tried something again, Hestin would be there to see that he failed.

The two men were hanged a week later, after a brief trial. Half the town testified against them, including Holly, who admitted her role in Archibald's schemes. All except for the shots she had taken at Horace Goodstone. Hestin had not mentioned seeing her that day. It was simpler not to, given he would then have to explain why he hadn't arrested her, something he could not even do to himself.

Better to ensure the two men hanged than to provide an opening for them to wiggle free, he told himself, though he did not entirely believe it. The whole thing left him feeling false and uncomfortable, compromised in some way that he could not quite define. Faced with a choice between bending and being broken, he had chosen the former, but he was still not certain it was the correct choice.

His outlook improved after the two were hanged and Sergeant Nettlecamp and McCauley left for Calgary. Nettlecamp left two constables behind, with Hestin in charge, to see to the rebuilding of the detachment. The town itself was quiet, and aside from a few of the usual incidents with miners, there was little for Hestin to be concerned with. Peace seemed to have come to the river valley.

There was still Holly Amos to consider, and on that matter, Hestin found himself as unsure and unsettled as ever. He did not trust her. She was a thief and, most likely, a murderer, though he could not prove it. She had worked for Gene Archibald as a hired gun, and Hestin had no doubt she would do the same for the next Gene Archibald who rode into town. But she had saved his life twice, and had risked her own facing down Archibald and Jeremiah James alone.

Did those acts balance out the others? They couldn't, Hestin knew. And yet...

Two weeks after the trial and hanging, Hestin came down to breakfast in the Rose Hotel. Holly would often join him for those meals, something he had grudgingly come to realize he looked forward to. That morning she did not, and he asked Ann Galvert if she had seen her.

"Didn't she tell you? She paid up her bill and checked out first light this morning. I expect she's well on her way now."

Hestin opened his mouth, about to ask her if Holly had said where she was going. Instead, he stopped himself, telling himself it was for the best that she was gone. It didn't feel that way though.

"She was quite the woman, wasn't she?" Ann Galvert said.

"She was," Hestin said and returned to his breakfast.

IF YOU ENJOYED
THE ADVENTURES OF
HOLLY AMOS,
YOU MIGHT ALSO LIKE:

THE DEVIOUS KIND

The body of a local woman is found in a coulee on a ranch north of Loverna, her head blown off with a shotgun. New to town and the job, Constable Martin Thomas arrives on the scene as a spring snowstorm begins to wipe out all evidence before his investigation has even begun.

There is no shortage of suspects to consider. A spurned husband. A jealous lover. A betrayed business partner. And family members battling over an inheritance. All have motive and opportunity. And no one seems to be telling him everything.

As he tries to sift the truth from the lies, the snowstorm continues to build, leaving Loverna cut off from the outside world. And Thomas alone to face a killer who will do anything not to get caught.

1

The body lay, sprawled awkwardly, partway down the coulee, right before the slope turned sheer and plunged to the creek far below. The night had hidden it, but the arrival of dawn made its presence obvious. There were several sets of footprints from where the body lay to the road, clearly marked in the muddy spring ground. Even as the new day's light revealed these details, the first flakes of snow began to fall, wet and heavy. For a time the earth resisted their intrusion, but eventually the storm proved too much and the ground turned white, covering over the tracks.

Wayne Johnstone noticed the body later that morning. By then the snow had covered all but the person's red jacket, which stood out vividly against the backdrop of white snow and the drab browns and greys of late March on the Canadian prairies. There was no green yet anywhere, not even any buds on the trees, spring only tentatively taking hold. The arrival of the storm promised that winter would not yet go quietly.

Even still he almost missed it, distracted by his worry about the storm's arrival. He had one hundred fifty cows still to calve and they were coming in bunches now. If the storm was as big as promised—and it looked to be, the snow descending so thickly he sometimes had trouble making out the highway—then he would likely lose some calves today.

There was little he could do about it, but it still worked at his thoughts, as he drove the tractor into the far pen where he turned out the cows who had already calved. Many were already tucked into the slat-fenced shelter near the gate, but they followed him deeper into the pen, heads low against the snow, waiting for the feed to emerge from the tub grinder.

It was as he reached the end of the first row of feed, and turned the tractor around to start the second, that he caught sight of the red jacket. Thinking it was something that had come off a passing car, he drove to the edge of the pen by the lip of the slope to see what it might be. Something in him recognized just what and who it was immediately, and he sat in the tractor, his hands clutching the steering wheel, feeling very cold.

After a time he clambered down the hillside, now slick with the accumulating snow, to confirm his suspicions. He stood looking down at her, the snow gathering on his shoulders and hat, before he managed to gather himself and return to the tractor. He reached into his pocket for his cell phone to call Diane, but stopped himself. Somehow it didn't seem right announcing this to her over the phone. He got back into the tractor and finished up with the last row for the cattle, before returning to the house.

He left the tractor running and went inside. Diane was in the kitchen lingering over her last cup of coffee. He called her from the entryway and she ducked her head around the corner to look at him, a frown on her face, knowing there had to be something wrong for him to have come in so soon after leaving.

"I just found Kristi Taid's body in the coulee," he said after a moment's hesitation. Saying the words made it feel much more real.

Diane seemed to not understand. "What's she doing out there?"

"She's dead," Wayne said with a heavy sigh. "Shotgun to the head."

"Oh," Diane said, reflecting and staring off glassy-eyed into the distance. "Better call the police, I guess."

Wayne was already fishing into his pocket to remove his cell phone. "Do you have the number?"

"Well, just 911, right? This has to be an emergency. My God, poor Leonard. I wonder if Clarissa's home."

Wayne nodded, realizing he had never in his life called the emergency line before. He stared at the flip phone in his hands, pulling it open gingerly, still unsure of the device. Diane had insisted he get one in case of emergencies, but the phone did not feel comfortable in his hands. Using it was still not intuitive. Briefly, he found himself wondering if he needed to dial a different emergency number for cell phones only, before dismissing that as ridiculous. Now he dialed and waited, listening to the ring.

"I'm going to call Leonard," Diane said.

"Don't," Wayne said, as the operator began to speak. "The police won't like that."

"I have to," Diane said.

Wayne knew better than to argue. He talked with the operator, telling what he had seen, and was told the constable would be on his way shortly. The detachment was in Loverna, Wayne knew, half an hour away. Probably more in the snow. He had time enough to get a few of the chores done before this new storm descended upon him, and he headed out the door to do so.

2

Half an hour later, a police car drove slowly up the driveway into the main yard, pulling to a stop in front of the ranch house, where Diane stood on the porch, a dog at her feet and a hood thrown over her head to keep off the snow.

"Hello, Diane," Constable Martin Tomas said as he stepped out of the car.

She just nodded. "It's down there by the coulee," she said, pointing. "You can take your car if you think it can make it through the mud."

"I'll be all right."

She paused, and then said, "We called him. Wayne said I probably shouldn't, but I had to."

He nodded. "He's down there now?"

"Yeah."

Martin got back into his car and drove slowly down the laneway that led to the far pens that edged onto the coulee. He went past pens filled with cattle still heavy with their winter coats, but he paid them no mind. Even six months ago he might have, but now, a year and a half into his term here, a cow was just a cow.

He arrived at the gate to the far corral, and could see Wayne's truck, a brand new 2003 Dodge Ram, parked by the fence and, on the other side, two figures staring down at the ground. Martin knew what they were looking at. He debated driving his car through the pen, but decided it was a poor idea. The ground would be soft in there, and the last thing he needed on a day like this was to get stuck in a corral.

It would have been easier, he realized, peering through the snow, if he had gone out to the highway and parked there, coming down through the ditch to the coulee. That was likely what had happened with whoever had killed Kristi Taid. With that thought, he reversed course and went out to the highway, parking his car on the shoulder and putting his hazards on, hoping that anyone who happened down the road would be able to see enough to spot them.

He stepped and slid his way from the road down into the ditch and from there made his way gingerly down the incline toward the coulee. A fence ran along the highway, ending at the coulee's edge, and Martin found himself wondering why Wayne hadn't bothered to extend it further. The coulee was part of his land and there was a pasture down below, but likely there was a fence somewhere there to keep the cattle from it.

Not that the cattle would be likely to ever make there way from the ravine's bottom up the highway. Even from its edge, Martin could not make out the coulee's bottom, could not see the creek that twisted and wound its way through its narrow passes. Trees, short and narrow-trunked, like all prairie trees, lined either side, obscuring what lay within.

The two men, both with lean rancher's frames made bulky by the winter clothes they were wearing, were watching as he approached. Martin could not make out their expressions through the swirl of the snow falling, for which he was oddly glad. He set his shoulders and nodded at them.

"Hello, Martin. Thanks for coming," Wayne said. He was a tall man, and would have been gangly in his youth.

Age had thickened him somewhat and now, in his early sixties, he appeared as a solid presence beside the more sleight Leonard, still powerful, in spite of his age.

"No problem," Martin said, an automatic reply, which sounded stupid, given the situation.

The other man, hood up on his jacket, hunched over to better keep his face clear of snow, did not say anything. His eyes had not strayed from the ground where the body lay. Martin looked at him carefully, now that he was up close, but his expression was blank. He seemed not to even realize that someone else had arrived on the scene. Well, it was his wife on the ground, after all.

Wayne moved aside so that Martin could get near the body. Martin stepped in, smiling his thanks and crouched over the body. The face was mostly blown away. He could see the outline of one eye socket and most of the jaw, bits of brain and skull. Her neck and chest were perforated with pellet blasts. The blood was that curdled dark color, clumping against her skin and the earth below. He sighed and stood up, turning to Leonard.

"It's her, all right," Leonard said. "That's her jacket and shoes."

Martin looked at Wayne. "Anybody else been down here but you two?"

Wayne shook his head.

"All right. Why don't you and Leonard head back to the house and wait for me? I want to look around a bit. Cory should be here pretty quick."

"What'll they do with the body?" Leonard asked, his tone odd.

"He'll have to take it into town. Botha will have to look at it. We'll take care of it."

He turned and knelt again by the body. The two others remained where they were, as though unsure of whether they should in fact leave, before Wayne reached out and put an arm on Leonard's shoulder and led him back to the pen. Martin looked up from the body, not leaving his crouch, and watched them get into Wayne's truck and drive back through the corral, the tires leaving clear tracks in the snow.

An eerie quiet descended around him, a product of the stillness that seemed to always come with a snowfall. The only sounds that intruded on his study of the body were the wind cutting through the coulee and the odd cow calling out to a calf in the pen beside him. He could hear his own breathing, which sounded hushed, as if even he did not want to disturb this scene.

It had already been disturbed, though; the snow had seen to that. The body had been dragged here, likely from the highway, given the lack of blood surrounding her and the severity of the gunshot wounds. The snow had already obscured any evidence of that passage, as well as the footprints of whoever had carried her here. There was also the matter of the remainder of her head, which was no doubt in pieces wherever she had been shot.

Where had she been shot and why had she been brought here? He stood up and found himself looking in the direction of the Taid's ranch. It did not make sense that Leonard would bring her here if he wanted to direct attention away from himself, given his home was only a mile away. And if someone else were trying to point the finger in his direction, they would be more likely to make sure her body was found somewhere on his land.

This felt more like an idea that had occurred in passing as the killers rushed to hide the trail that led to them. Dump the body in the coulee and hope the storm, which everyone had known was coming, would hide the body. If they had gotten her farther down into the coulee it very well might have, Martin realized. And if the coyotes had gotten to the body, it might have been a very long time indeed before any trace was found of her.

Which led to another question: why here? Why not take the body down farther and deeper into the trees? The body lay between two short, shrub-like trees, but without their leaves the body was exposed to both the road and the pen. Whoever had done it was in a rush, working in the dark so that Wayne and Diane didn't chance to see them, perhaps struggling with weight of the corpse. They had come this far and judged it far enough. What had led to that haste, and where had they been going initially before they changed their plans and chose this place to hide the body?

He paced from the body back to the road. The only tracks leading into the ditch were his own, and even they were rapidly disappearing. He climbed back up onto the highway, kicking at the damp blacktop. Soon it too would surrender to the snow, disappearing beneath it. The road curved just ahead along with the coulee, the two running nearly parallel briefly, before it curved again to wrap around the valley. The snow was coming down so heavily he could not see beyond that.

He went back to the body, snapping on the rubber gloves he had brought as he went, feeling faintly ridiculous as he did so. This was his first murder investigation, and he was very conscious of making a misstep and also of being found out for a fraud. That, as much as anything else, had been why he sent Wayne and Leonard away. Though obviously Leonard was very much a suspect, Martin could not have both of them around further contaminating the crime scene.

All he knew about conducting this sort of investigation he had learned at the academy in Regina, though the principles were the same as with any of the dozens of robberies and assaults he had been called in on while here or in Wetaskawin, where he had been stationed previously. It did not feel that way now that he was faced with a dead body. This felt of much greater import. A life had been lost, after all. And it fell to him to determine who had been responsible.

Wiping his eyes clear of water and snow, he knelt down and gingerly turned what was left of Kristi's head toward him and pulled back her remaining eyelid. The eye beneath was cloudy and the body itself stiff with rigor mortis, no doubt helped by the temperature, which had hovered around the freezing mark for most of the night through to the morning.

Martin stood, clicking his tongue against the roof of his mouth thoughtfully, and started to pull his gloves off when he heard a vehicle approaching. He watched as the ambulance pulled up behind his car and Cory slid his bulk out from behind the wheel. The ambulance driver wandered over, his jeans tucked into unlaced work boots, his jacket open to the elements as well. He was unshaven and, as he came up alongside, Martin caught a whiff of booze.

"Late night?"

"Oh," Cory said with a wave of his hand. His eyes were bloodshot, but that was hardly surprising for Cory. In spite of the fact they were both in their early thirties, Martin always thought of Cory as being much younger. He certainly acted like it.

"You good to drive yet?"

"I made it here, didn't I?"

"Don't make me put the fucking Breathalyzer on you," Martin said. "I've got enough shit to deal with without you cocking things up."

Cory waved his hand again and turned his attention to the body. "Kristi Taid."

"Yes," Martin said.

"Cause of death shouldn't be a problem, anyway."

"No."

"Well, how you wanna do this? Bring the stretcher down from the highway, probably the easiest."

Martin agreed, and they both made their way up the ditch to the back of the ambulance, where they offloaded the stretcher. Together they wheeled it down into the ditch and gingerly set Kristi's body upon it. Beneath where her body had lain was only dormant grass and dead leaves. No doubt he was ruining all kinds of forensic evidence, but who knew how long it would take for the RCMP to send a forensics team out. The storm would only complicate things further, and Martin could not just leave the body here for all the world driving by to see.

Once the body was safely strapped to the stretcher, they wheeled it back up the ditch, both of them slipping and cursing on the slope. When they had the stretcher safely into the back of the ambulance, Cory turned to Martin.

"Take it in to Botha, then?"

"Yes," Martin said. "And for fuck's sake, Cory, don't phone anyone, don't let anyone know. This is an RCMP investigation now."

Cory didn't reply, giving him another wave, and was on his way. Martin sighed and swore again under his breath. He stood and watched until the ambulance had disappeared in the snow. He waited before getting into his own car, looking up at the vast wall of grey clouds above him, already thinking of the questions he would have to ask Leonard.

THE DEVIOUS KIND is now available.

ABOUT THE AUTHOR

Clint Westgard writes mystery, crime and western novels, as well as science fiction and fantasy. He has published a work of historical fantasy set in colonial Peru, The Maleficio Chronicles, and a retelling of the Minotaur legend, The Trials of the Minotaur. He lives in Calgary, Alberta.

ALSO BY CLINT WESTGARD

The Devious Kind

A Mystery

The body of a local woman is found in a coulee on a ranch
north of Loverna, her head blown off with a shotgun. New
to town and the job, Constable Martin Thomas arrives on
the scene as a spring snowstorm begins to wipe out all
evidence before his investigation has even begun.

There is no shortage of suspects to consider. A spurned
husband. A jealous lover. A betrayed business partner.
And family members battling over an inheritance. All have
motive and opportunity. And no one seems to be telling
him everything.

As he tries to sift the truth from the lies, the snowstorm
continues to build, leaving Loverna cut off from the
outside world. And Thomas alone to face a killer who will
do anything not to get caught.

ALSO BY CLINT WESTGARD

The Maleficio Chronicles

Luisa is always more than she appears. Rumor and mystery surround her. And strange events seem to follow wherever she goes.

Born in Lima, City of Kings, to a noble family, her father so fears her true nature that he banishes her to a convent. There she falls under the suspicion of the Inquisition and decides to flee.

Disguised as a man, she embarks upon a series of wild adventures, dueling, carousing, and gambling her way across colonial Peru. But everything changes when someone recognizes her for what she truly is, and soon she finds herself fighting for her very survival.

In a world where she will always stand apart, Luisa undergoes a strange journey, marked by betrayal and murder, terrible powers and mysterious strangers. *The Maleficio Chronicles* is her incredible confession and a story like no other.

ALSO BY CLINT WESTGARD

The Trials of the Minotaur

In the fifth year of the rule of Auten the One Eyed a minotaur is born to one of Colosi's most important families.

Taken from his mother as a newborn, exiled and cast from his family, the minotaur vows to return to the imperial city and take his rightful place as a patrician in the empire. But the patriarch of the family, his grandfather, will stop at nothing to see this blemish to his honor destroyed.

And so begins an epic journey, through lands beyond imagining, marked by despair and exile, triumph and betrayal. At its heart lies a quest to be free.

ALSO BY CLINT WESTGARD

The Forgotten
Volume One of The Sojourners Cycle

Who is David Aeida? And what does he know that has so
many people pursuing him?

David doesn't know. He can't remember anything about
who he is. But he finds himself ensnared in a vicious
conflict between a religious cult and a guild that patrols the
crossings between multiple universes. They will both stop
at nothing to gain whatever knowledge he possesses. Most
dangerous of all, is the implacable hunter, known only as
the Seeker, who has his own reasons for wanting to find
David.

His only hope is to recover his memories before they do.
His only ally is a woman named Merecith, and she
definitely knows more than she is telling…

Spanning both universes and the human mind, The
Forgotten is an unforgettable science fiction thriller that
questions the very nature of identity. It is the first volume
of the Sojourners Cycle, an epic that will encompass the
fates of universes and humanity itself.

ALSO BY CLINT WESTGARD

The Apostate
Volume Two of The Sojourners Cycle

Laila has only one goal in mind. To have her revenge upon
the Grand Regent for all he has done to her. First, though,
she needs to find her way across the universes.

That is easier said than done. The Grand Regent's agents
are still pursuing her. As is the Society of Travellers. And
the Seeker lurks somewhere, waiting for his moment to
strike.

Laila has a plan, though, and a few tricks of her own. But
she will discover that not everything is at seems. For the
war she has given her life to hides a far greater conflict.

Spanning multiple universes and the complexities of the
human mind, The Apostate, continues the incredible
journey begun in The Forgotten. The second volume of
The Sojourners Cycle is an unforgettable science fiction
epic that encompasses the fates of universes and humanity
itself.

ALSO BY CLINT WESTGARD

The Acolyte
Volume Three of The Sojourners Cycle

After crossing the universes to join with Toma Osahi's group of renegades in their battle for control of the Church of Regents, Laila finds herself in a precarious position. While they both share the same goal—the destruction of the Grand Regent—Osahi doesn't know who Laila really is. What will he do if he finds out?

While Laila struggles to keep her identity secret, Osahi and his people pull her deeper and deeper into a search for Ana that promises to shed light on the dark secrets of the Watchers' Order and the Acolytes. Before she can find those answers though, Laila will have to face what lies within.

Crossing the universes has unsettled the already shaky equilibrium in her mind. If she wants to return herself to her own body, she will have to act fast, for the consequences of what Acolytes did to her are still reverberating. And Aeida hides somewhere, waiting for his time to come.

The thrilling third volume of the Sojourners Cycle continues Laila's incredible journey across the universes against incredible odds, as well as exploring her past, including the pivotal role she played in the rise of the Grand Regent and her own downfall at his hands.

ALSO BY CLINT WESTGARD

The Double
Volume Four of The Sojourners Cycle

David Aeida now commands his body, having cast Laila
aside. He has sworn fealty to the Grand Regent, who
wants him by his side and sees that his loyalty is rewarded.

But the Grand Regent is not the man he was. He is
paranoid and suspicious of everyone, isolated in his tower,
and thirsting for vengeance against those he feels have
wronged him. How long until he turns on Aeida as well?

That is only the beginning of Aeida's problems. For he
knows the Seeker and the Society of Travelers remain to
play their parts. Both desire nothing more than the utter
destruction of the Church of Regents and all its works.
And though Laila has been defeated, he knows better than
anyone not to assume she has been vanquished.

The epic fourth volume of the Sojourners Cycle centers
upon the many betrayals and lies at the heart of the faith of
the Church of Regents and the devastation upon the lives
of the faithful they have wrought. Desire and guilt, love
and revenge, rage and despair will drive them all, with
consequences for all the universes.

ALSO BY CLINT WESTGARD

The Sojourner
Volume Five of The Sojourners Cycle

Laila's strange and reluctant alliance with the Seeker
continues, though she does not know where it will lead
her. She fears it will place her in another prison, worse
than the one she has just managed to escape.

But her escape is not entirely complete. For though she
has been restored to her own flesh, parts of Aeida
somehow still remain. Along with some other she does not
recognize. Is this some aftereffect of the Acolyte's bizarre
procedure? Or the result of the Seeker's meddling?

All this pales in comparison to what Laila soon discovers.
That she has an unwanted part to play in an ancient
struggle for who will rule the crossings between the
universes and all that lies in them.

In the stunning conclusion to the Sojourners Cycle Laila
will be faced with a terrible choice, one that will decide her
fate and humanity's.

ALSO BY CLINT WESTGARD

Realm of Shadows
Volume One of The Shadow Men

Craitol and Renuih, two empires a world apart, divided by the desert that lies between them. A desert ruled by the Shadow Men.

An uneasy peace holds sway in both realms, hiding longstanding feuds and bitter rivalries. Until a Shadow Men raid on Renuih shatters the calm and sets in motion events no one can control.

Masiph id Ezern, unfavored son of the Imperial Vazeir, finds himself a hero following the raid. His father remains unmoved by his exploits and, in his bitterness, Masiph will find himself a reluctant participant in a plot against the empire.

As he finds himself drawn deeper and deeper into the conspiracy, he soon realizes there will be no escaping the realm of shadows, where intrigue and betrayal abound. And though the Shadow Men have gone quiet, they will not stay silent forever…

ALSO BY CLINT WESTGARD

Council of Shadows
Volume Two of The Shadow Men

Discontent continues to fester within the realms of Craitol and Renuih, fed by intrigues carried out in the shadows. As rivals and apostates struggle for supremacy, a long incubated plan begins to unfold.

Vyissan, a mysterious alkemycal practitioner arrives in Renuih, the latest strike in a long war over who shall control the secrets of alkemya and Craitol itself. He carries with him a secret that, once revealed, will reverberate across all realms. Before he can reveal it though, the conspirators against the emperor will strike their own blow.

But now, a new and more powerful menace looms on the horizon. The Shadow Men have gained the secrets of the Council Adept's alkemya and no one can be certain what they will do with it...

ALSO BY CLINT WESTGARD

Dance of Shadows
Volume Three of The Shadow Men

War with the Shadow Men looms in both realms as the
consequences of the Gvers' Council in Craitol begin to
make themselves known. A war that could end in glorious
triumph or bitter disaster.

Doubt shadows everyone's steps, for they know there are
no certainties in the desert. Especially now the Shadow
Men have made the art of alkemya their own.

No one has more questions than Vyissan, for he is
working in service to a cause he is no longer sure he
believes in. And now he must undertake a journey with
those who both loathe and fear him. Before the first sword
is drawn, his life will be under threat.

But his will not be the only one, for somewhere in the
desert the Shadow Men lie in wait.